MW01245967

WHAT'S UP DOCTOR?

LACY EMBERS

HIDDEN KEY PUBLISHING

WHAT'S UP DOCTOR is a work of fiction. Names, characters, places, and incidents are products of the creator's imagination or used fictitiously. Any resemblance to actual events, locales, or persons, living or dead, is entirely coincidental.

1

Ross Hardwick took another sip of champagne and managed to avoid making eye contact with Julia Christianson across the rather crowded art gallery, despite her efforts to attract his attention. He supported the charity wholeheartedly, but here was a reason he hated these galas. It seemed that many people had forgotten the reason for the gala and were more focused on trying to get him on a date.

Not that Ross was above taking someone home, but he was only interested in one night of pleasure, and they inevitably wanted more. It came with having a relatively large price tag attached to his name, he supposed. At times like these he wished he was still poor and anonymous. But he couldn't regret his success for long, not when he could throw his financial weight and medical expertise behind organizations like Hearts in Hands.

Hearts in Hands was his favorite of the few charities that he supported. Most charities, such as World Wildlife Fund, he donated to every year around Christmas. A select few, usually those with a medical bent such as local cancer foundations, received more frequent donations from him, along with his occasional presence at a fundraiser. But Hearts in Hands dealt specifically with funding research into heart diseases and the life-saving medical care that heart patients couldn't otherwise afford. Ross had done extensive research into their board of directors, founders, history, budget, and spending when he'd considered donating to them, and he had yet to be disappointed. He may have chosen to be a surgeon, but heart disease was an issue that meant a lot to him, and he was glad to be able to fund efforts to ensure that heart patients received the care they desperately needed regardless of their financial situation.

He supposed that getting hit on by women (and the occasional man) was worth suffering through if it meant that he got to throw his weight behind such a good cause.

Ross turned towards one of the paintings on the wall and pretended to be avidly studying it. Normally his interest in the painting would be genuine, seeing as it was an exhibition on the Cubists and he was a fan, but for the moment his mind was occupied with plans to escape Julia.

He turned to survey the exits, and found his gaze snagging on someone he'd never seen before. Being a huge contributor to Hearts in Hands, he generally knew who their biggest donors were. He was friends with everyone on the board, and he tended to see the same people at these galas. But this woman was new, and intriguing. She was tall, and her hair was a cascading mess of light red ringlets. She had somehow arranged those tight bouncing curls in such a way that they looked wild while still retaining a lovely shape around her heart-shaped face. It was her eyes that kept him looking, though. Not merely for their lovely light blue-green coloring, but the unmistakable look of trepidation in them. The poor woman looked out of her element. In fact, she looked rather like Ross felt.

Well, never let it be said that he didn't come to a woman's rescue when needed.

Ross crossed the room, surprised that, despite his rather obvious beeline for her, the woman didn't seem to notice him until he was right at her elbow. "Excuse me."

The woman jumped and turned to look at him, her hand tightening on her glass of champagne. "Can I help you?" Her voice was light and airy, but in a false way, as if she were forcing it to sound helpful. Ross had heard that tone plenty of times from workers in customer service. Hell, he'd heard it in his own voice back when he'd been working as a waiter.

"Actually, I was wondering if I could help you." He smiled in what he hoped was a reassuring fashion.

The woman smiled back at him, but her eyebrows drew together in confusion. "I'm sorry?"

"You seemed a little lost," Ross explained. "And I'm in dire need of a conversation partner."

"Oh, no, I'm..." Her voice trailed off and she looked around the room, as if looking for something. Her gaze slid back to him. "Sorry, I'm being rude. I'm Sharon Talcott, new head of PR for Hearts in Hands."

Come to think of it, he did vaguely recall someone mentioning that the charity had hired someone new. Hard worker, first big gig, something like that.

Sharon held out her hand for him to shake. Ross took it, noting how much smaller her hands were than his. Her grip was strong, though. Small but strong. He liked that. He held Sharon's hand and gaze a little longer than strictly necessary, noting with pleasure how her breath seemed to catch in her throat. She really was lovely. Her dark green dress brought out the color of her eyes and complimented the fire of her hair. If only he could smooth away the tightness in her shoulders and the tense set of her jaw. Then again, perhaps he could.

"I thought I heard that H-I-H was hiring someone new. Congratulations."

Sharon snorted and dropped his hand. "Congratulate me after this gala goes well."

"First time organizing one of these?" Ross snagged some hors d'oeuvres and offered one to Sharon. She smiled up at him, her entire face lighting up, and Ross felt warmth spread in his chest. Sappy, of course, but his pleasure in helping people was part of why he'd become a surgeon.

"My first time with this organization. Everything's on a much… more expensive scale than I'm used to." Sharon gave him a small smile, one that seemed surprisingly self-deprecating. "This was practically my first task once I took on the position and I haven't really had time to get used to anything yet."

"I've been to a lot of these things," Ross said, "And I can promise you that you did well. I appreciate the choice of gallery."

Sharon's smile grew, lighting up her entire face again. She really was attractive. And in she appeared to be in need of de-stressing. Ross smiled. "Are you a fan of Cubist art?"

"I'm afraid I'm more of an Impressionist girl." Sharon sounded like she was under valuing herself again, her voice dipping down. "Renoir, Monet, that sort."

"You don't have to sound ashamed of it." Ross offered his arm. "I can talk to you about it, if you'd like. You'd be saving my ass, anyway."

"I'd be saving you?" Sharon laughed. "Sounds like it's the other way around."

She took his arm, and Ross began to lead her around the room. "So why do you need rescuing?" She asked.

Ross swallowed. It seemed silly to say it out loud. "At these gatherings people tend to… take it as an opportunity to try and solicit me for dates."

"Oh no, you're handsome and rich, how awful," Sharon teased. Her eyes widened as soon as she said it, like she was a little horrified at herself. Ross didn't know if she was horrified for teasing him so soon or for admitting that she thought he was handsome, but either way he liked that she'd said it.

He gave her arm a light squeeze. "You think I'm handsome?"

"I suspect you know that, since you have all these people clamoring to be your date."

"I'm not saying I was unaware of my looks, I'm asking if you like them."

"Maybe." Sharon looked up at him through her lashes, a little coy, and Ross felt his grin turn wolfish. "What's so bad about going on a date? You might be surprised at how much you like the person."

"I'm not interested in dating at the moment. I've got too much else on my plate." *And I'm not making the mistake of dating again*, he thought but didn't add. That was far too long a story to get into right now, and far too personal to discuss with someone he'd just met, no matter how pretty she was.

Sharon nodded. "I understand that. I've got a lot going on too, adjusting to this new job. Nobody has time."

"Especially if the date doesn't work out, then it's hours wasted."

Sharon gave a little shudder. "Or they turn out to be creeps."

"I hope I'm not giving you that impression."

Sharon looked up at him through her lashes again. "So far you're doing well."

"So far?"

"Well you haven't compared me to previous exes or talked to me like I'm a doll that's just supposed to nod and agree with everything you say."

Ross chuckled. He'd observed more than a few dates going that way, seeing the man go on and on while the woman was forced to just nod and smile in a pained sort of way. "Isn't nodding and smiling a big part of PR?"

Sharon snorted. "Some people seem to think so. It pisses them off when I put my foot down. PR is about taking care of your company and your company's image, and sometimes that means going to bat for your company. It means being willing to take the heat when some big shot at the company gets drunk and appears in the tabloids, or a celebrity that worked with you goes to rehab, or somebody embezzles. I mean, yeah, there's a lot of making nice and more ass kissing than I'd like, but it doesn't mean I don't have a backbone."

Her voice took on a firmer tone as she spoke. If this was how she acted in the office and with clients, Ross could see why HiH had hired her. "I like your conviction."

Sharon blushed faintly, and Ross filed that observation away for use later. Good at her job, sure of her abilities, but stressed out by the gala. Firm in her stance, yet easily embarrassed by compliments. What a lovely set of contradictions.

"Dating can be a risk, of course," he went on, "I've always preferred skipping right to the end of the night, if both parties are interested." He let his gaze travel down her body, taking in her lithe frame and long legs.

Sharon's blush deepened, but after a moment she raised her head to meet his gaze. "And are you interested?"

"I think that I'd be flattered to take a beautiful woman like you home for the night."

"You'd be flattered?" Sharon laughed. "The guy that everyone else is clamoring to date would be the flattered one if we hooked up."

"Sharon." Ross tipped his head at the room around them. "Do me a favor and take a look around. I'd say there are at least five men in here glaring at me because I got to you before they did."

In fact, he gave one of those men a level stare as they passed by. The man in question was Lewis Malchire, another one of HiH's big donors. Ross ordinarily didn't have anything against Lewis who was a big football fan and had a good sense of humor but he wanted to make it clear that nobody else would be muscling in on Sharon. Not tonight, anyway. Although, if things went well tonight, she could become a regular hookup. It would make these galas easier to endure, anyway.

Hold on, what? He hadn't even gotten the woman into bed with him yet and he was considering making this a regular thing? Ross clenched his jaw and cleared his thoughts.

"You're exaggerating." Sharon glanced hurriedly around the room, as if afraid everyone would know what she was thinking as she did it.

"You're stressed," Ross noted, taking in how her shoulders stiffened.

Sharon nodded. "As I said, first big gala."

"Let me help you ease some of that. Get that tension out of your body."

Sharon looked over at him. "I can't tell if you're serious or not. Men don't usually... just come up like this."

"I believe in cutting right to the chase." He reached up, tucking one of her tight curls behind her ear. He let his fingers trail along her jaw as he did so, and he saw her inhale shakily. He lowered his voice. "I'm sure no one would mind if you ducked out just a little early."

Sharon glanced around again, this time a little guiltily. "I don't want anyone to think I'm skipping out."

"You set this whole thing up. And I'm betting you've got an assistant who can handle closing duties."

Sharon ran her teeth over her lower lip. Ross wanted to lean in and bite into it - turn that stress into something exciting and erotic. He turned her until they were both facing a painting, ostensibly to discuss it, but really so that he had an excuse to slip his arm around her waist. He leaned in close enough for his lips to brush the shell of her ear as he murmured, "Let's turn something boring and stressful into something fun, shall we?"

Sharon shivered. Ross let his thumb swipe slowly along the fabric encircling her waist. "I'll admit it's... tempting," Sharon said.

"You're tempting."

She inhaled again at that, a shaky breath that made her pulse flutter in her throat. Ross wanted to put his lips there, his tongue, maybe even his teeth, scraping lightly along the column of her neck...

"Okay." Sharon nodded. "O-okay. Sure. Let's go back to your place."

Ross grinned, baring his teeth in a way that he knew made him look rather predatory. Sharon turned her head just in time to see it, and Ross had the pleasure of seeing her pupils dilate in response.

He took a small step back, putting some space between them, and pointed to the exit. Sharon let out a breath, her eyes a bit wide. Oh, he was going to have fun taking her apart. Maybe he could even get her to scream.

She disappeared into the crowd for a moment, undoubtedly to talk to her assistant. Ross waited near the door. Hopefully some guest wouldn't suck Sharon into a conversation, or Sharon's assistant wouldn't be upset about being asked to take over. It reminded him of when he was with Amanda, always waiting on her, always playing second fiddle to her latest possible scoop or story. Sometimes she'd stand him up because she was 'tracking down a lead.' At the time, he hadn't wanted to complain, knowing how much her career meant to her. After all, his job as a surgeon meant that there were times he had to drop everything to rush in and help a patient. But that sick, restless feeling, that feeling of being left behind like a toy or a pet to just wait until Amanda returned…

He shook himself a little. It amazed him, really, how the memories still rose up and clung to him after all of this time. It wasn't PTSD he would never presume to call it that but in moments like these, the feeling of being used and manipulated was still fresh and raw.

Thank God he didn't have to deal with any of that anymore. Now he had simplicity. And for tonight he had Sharon, who was making her way back to him through the crowd. She looked a little flushed, and there was a gleam in her eye that Ross recognized from his previous hook-ups: the thrill of doing something bad.

"She said she's fine with it," Sharon said. She smiled tentatively up at Ross, the edges of her mouth wavering around it like she was still unsure that this was the right thing.

"See? Told you," Ross said. "You deserve to duck out a little early. Trust me, there's going to be plenty of nights where you'll be stuck here for hours. HiH might not be too well known outside of Pittsburgh, but this is a big city and they host a lot of events."

"They're not too well known outside of Pittsburgh yet," Sharon corrected. Ambitious then. Ross bit hard on the inside of his cheek to keep from smiling, sure that Sharon would mistake his delight for condescension. HiH needed someone with ambition like hers to get them onto the national stage.

Not to mention that Ross had found that ambition and confidence translated well into the bedroom. He was definitely looking forward to this encounter. Good thing he didn't live far.

They gathered their coats and Ross let Sharon lead him to her car.

He'd taken a taxi to the gala since he never knew when he'd be too tipsy to drive home. Better safe than sorry.

The car ride was quiet, broken only by Ross giving Sharon directions to his apartment just a couple of blocks away, but it wasn't without tension. He put his hand on her leg once they'd buckled themselves in, and when Sharon hadn't moved it, he'd slowly slid it higher as she drove. He could feel the heat radiating off of her, her hands gripping the steering wheel so tightly that her knuckles were white. By the time they parked he could brush his fingertips along the lace of her underwear, her dress hiked up around her creamy legs. He could feel the minute tremble in her body every time he moved his hand up, her tremors fueling the heat inside him. He wanted to see if she was wet yet, and wondered if, had the drive only been longer, she'd have spread her thighs and let him move his hand higher, perhaps even letting him slip his fingers underneath the hem of her underwear...

Sharon threw the car into park. "Th-this is it, 254, like you said."

Ross glanced out the window. It was, in fact, his apartment complex. "Excellent parking skills."

He noticed that Sharon's mouth twitched in response, almost as though she were trying to hide a pleased smile. So, she liked praise. Useful information.

Ross got out and hurried around the car to open the door for her, offering a hand to help her stand. Sharon took it, but he didn't let go once the car door was closed, intertwining their fingers so he could lead her. The night doorman, Jose, was working on a crossword as they passed. "Gala went well, Dr. H?"

"Better than usual," Ross replied, giving Sharon's hand a squeeze. She kept her eyes on the ground, as though she thought Jose would judge them. Jose had seen plenty of Ross's hookups over the years, though, and if he did judge Ross for it he'd managed to do an excellent job of pretending otherwise. "Jose, this is Sharon. It's okay if she leaves her car outside, right?"

"Should be fine, but I'll get her a guest pass." Jose began rifling through the drawers for one. As he did so, Sharon raised her eyes and glanced at the crossword.

"Nasturtium."

Jose and Ross both looked at her. "What?"

"Nasturtium. 6 across, ten letter word for a low growing, edible, and brightly colored flower, often used in salads."

Ross stared at her. PR for a major charity, understood art, and good at crossword puzzles. He couldn't wait to get his hands on her. "Has anyone told you that you're quite intelligent?"

There it was again, the twist to her lips like she was hiding a smile. This time she blushed slightly as well. She definitely liked praise, then. Ross fully planned on taking advantage of that.

Jose emerged with the guest pass. "I'll put this on your windshield, if you'd like."

"Thanks, Jose." Ross gently led Sharon towards the elevator. "Have a good night."

"You too, Dr. H."

Once they got into the elevator, Ross wasted no time in crowding her up against the wall, his hands on her hips. He paused just for a moment, his face an inch from hers, just in case. To his pleasure, Sharon didn't pull away or stiffen, but rather she arched up into his touch, pressing her body up against his.

"I could devour you," he admitted. He ducked his head and ran his lips lightly over her pulse point before scattering a few kisses along her jaw.

Sharon's hands came up to grip his shoulders and she pressed herself closer to him, tilting her head so she could give him better access to her sweet-smelling skin. "Ross..." her voice sounded shaky and breathy. He loved it. "Ross, the... the elevator's stopped."

He pulled back a little and realized that it had. A second later, the doors opened. "I can't help it if you're distracting."

"I could argue that you were the one doing the distracting," Sharon replied, a teasing note in her voice. She darted past him into the hallway and crooked a finger at him.

Ross gave her another devilish grin and advanced on her, pleased with how her eyes went wide again. She let him grab her by the waist and pull her in. "I could argue that it's time I kissed you properly."

He ducked down, pressing their mouths together in a crushing kiss. Sharon's lips opened on a small gasp and he ran his tongue over her bottom lip. Sharon opened her mouth wider in response and let him slip his tongue inside. His tongue tangled with hers, and then he slowly moved in and out of her mouth, imitating what he wanted to do with her body. Sharon pulled back for a moment, gasping, but then pressed back in, letting him kiss her as deeply as he wanted. He kept at it, diving in again and again. He loved how pliant she was, how she pressed up against him and wound her arms around his neck, how she shuddered when he palmed her ass and hiked her up against his body. Her responsiveness drove him wild.

He needed to get her into his bed right now, or they might never make it that far. But he remembered how she'd let him take the lead, and her reaction to his praise, and he knew that if he could only hold onto his patience he'd have plenty of fun with her tonight.

Which actually reminded him... "Sharon." He pulled back. "I'm sorry I'm just now remembering to mention this. I usually ask right away. But I'm going to have to ask that you not stay the night."

Sharon blinked. Her gaze was hazy with lust, but then it cleared. Fortunately, she didn't seem put out. "No problem. Is it okay if I shower before I leave?"

"Yes, of course."

She nodded. "If that's all..." She moved her hands up to cradle his jaw, gently tilting his head so that she could press a kiss to the corner of his mouth. "How about you show me this apartment you keep swearing you have? I don't think your neighbors will be too happy if we give them a show."

"You never know, they might applaud." Ross grinned, then turned his head so he could intercept her next kiss and gently suck her bottom lip into his mouth. Finally, he forced himself to pull away. "C'mon."

He led her down the hallway to his apartment. Hastily he unlatched the door and ushered her in.

Sharon turned around delightedly in his entryway. "I'd love a tour!"

He stared at her blankly for a moment. Then a sly smile crept over her face and he realized that she was kidding. "You're a bit of a minx, you know."

"So I've been told." She winked at him.

Ross growled and advanced on her, ducking low to catch her around the legs and scoop her up. Sharon shrieked in delighted surprise, clutching his shoulders and laughing wildly as he carried her into the bedroom.

"What am I supposed to do with a minx like you?" He asked, depositing her on the bed.

Sharon bit her lip, trying to hold in her smile, but he could see it nonetheless. "I suppose you'll just have to make me behave, won't you?"

Ross was all for that idea.

"Move back." Sharon obligingly scooted back against the pillows so that Ross had room to crawl up the bed. He settled between her legs, before taking an ankle in each hand and pulling gently. Soon she was settled on her back below him, her legs spread wide.

Slowly, keeping eye contact with him, Sharon took the hem of her dress and raised it up. "I'll bet you'll want to see how wet you made me," she whispered, "teasing me in the car and then in the elevator."

Ross gripped her ankles and tried not to rip her dress off of her. It looked so lovely on her that it'd be a shame to rip it, but he was sorely tempted.

"Who's being the tease now?" he asked when Sharon stopped just before exposing herself completely.

"Maybe I want to see what you'll do."

Ahhh. She was baiting him, trying to get him to take control. Ross could do that. He'd do it and enjoy it.

"Take the dress off," he growled, lowering his voice. Sharon gave a delicious full-body shiver and followed his orders, raising the dress over her head and tossing it to the floor.

Ross hungrily took in the sight before him. Oh, she was gorgeous, with small breasts and creamy skin and underwear stained dark from her arousal. He was going to kiss every inch of that skin before the night was over.

"Nice bra," he remarked, raising an eyebrow before he reached down and dragged a thumb over her nipple. Sharon trembled and her eyelids fluttered.

"I couldn't wear one with this dress," she said, sounding slightly petulant.

Ross leaned closer and tugged lightly on her earlobe with his teeth. "Give yourself whatever excuse you want, Miss Talcott. I think it's rather scandalous."

Sharon made a delightful gasping, helpless noise at that. Ross kneaded her breast with one hand, swiping his thumb over it again. "All I had to do in that gala was slide my hand in and I could have touched you, just like this. What if we'd just found a dark corner and done it there, hmm? Would you have let me just hike up your dress and put you up against the wall?"

He could feel Sharon shaking, either with arousal or with the effort to remain still. Possibly both. Ross nuzzled into her neck. "You would let me, wouldn't you? You'd be a good girl for me, do whatever I told you to do?"

"Y-yes," Sharon whispered, and he could see her neck and chest flush with embarrassment. Now, that simply wouldn't do.

"I like that," he assured her. "Will you do what I ask you to do now?"

Ross pulled back a little so he could see her, and Sharon nodded. Ross smiled. Excellent.

He slid his hands up her legs, stopping just short of her lacy emerald green panties. His thumbs rubbed lazy circles into her skin. Sharon spread her legs even wider, her nails digging into the blankets on either side of her. "Now put your hands on the headboard," Ross instructed, gentling his voice but keeping it sultry.

Sharon's breath hitched and she reached up, gripping the slats in the headboard as tightly as she'd gripped the steering wheel earlier. Ross smiled down at her. "Good girl."

Sharon bit her lip hard, apparently to smother a gasp or smile. Ross leaned down and began to kiss along her stomach.

"You should get undressed," Sharon said. She still sounded a little wobbly but her voice was lower, like she was struggling to get it back under control. That wouldn't do.

"Not yet."

He kissed his way up her stomach, then took one of her breasts into his mouth, sucking at her nipple and then tugging at it lightly with his teeth. He delighted in the high whine that Sharon let out almost involuntarily. He swept up and kissed her on the mouth. "Keep holding on."

Sharon nodded, her hands gripping the slats more firmly. Ross ducked his head down to kiss along her thighs, pulling her silky underwear down as he did so. Christ, he could smell her, heady and intoxicating. He wasted no time in tasting her, tracing his tongue around her clit. Sharon keened again, arching up into his mouth. Ross gently placed his hands on her hips to hold her down. He could feel her trembling as he dove in, again and again. He added his fingers into the mix, first one, then two and moved them in counterpoint to his mouth. He listened carefully for the escalation of her soft cries, felt it when her legs drew back and stiffened, and realized that her body was bracing for orgasm.

He pulled back and looked up at her face.

Sharon was covered in sweat, her hair frizzing and sticking to her face, her eyes shining and glazed with lust. She looked absolutely beautiful.

She also looked a little confused. "Why… did you stop?"

Ross flashed his predatory grin and was rewarded by the sight of Sharon's hands flexing against the slats and the sound of her swallowed gasp. "Because I want you to come while I'm inside you."

Sharon gave a delicious full-body shiver. "Then why don't you get up here?"

Ross obliged her, sliding up her body and taking himself in hand. Sharon reached down and wrapped her hand around him, stroking him slowly. Ross closed his eyes and swallowed a groan. She moved slowly but surely, teasing him still. "Condoms?"

Ross forced himself to breathe evenly and reached over to the nightstand drawer, fishing out a condom and the small bottle of lube. "Okay, okay," he said, moving to prepare. "You sure you're good?"

Sharon gave him a look that would have melted a wall of concrete. "Dr. Ross I've-actually-forgotten-your-last-name, if you don't stop teasing and—"

He kissed her, lining himself up as he did so. "Feisty, aren't we?" He didn't give her a chance to respond. He was starting to enter her even as he finished the question.

Sharon gasped, her hands tightening on the slats. "Can I—please can I touch you?"

Ross waited until he was completely inside her. He bit his lip as he mastered the impulse to pull back and slam into her. She was so tight and hot, and he wanted to bury himself in her again and again. But first…

"Since you asked nicely."

Sharon let go of the headboard. She grabbed his shoulders and hauled him even closer, hooking one of her legs around his back as she arched up against him. Ross began to move, trying to go slowly at first, then faster as Sharon urged him on, whispering 'please, please, *please*' in his ear like it was the only thing she could remember how to say. God, she was so beautiful, arching up under him again and again and responding beautifully to his every move—especially when he found the angle that made her scream. Ross buried his face in her soft hair and kept moving inside her until she gave one last scream. Her nails dug into his back and he could feel her shuddering around him. He couldn't hold back then, thrusting wildly until he tipped over the edge. He nearly collapsed on her, his gasps almost matching hers.

2

After Ross told her that he didn't want her to spend the night, Sharon began to worry that it would be awkward after they'd finished what they came for. She hadn't ever had a one-night stand before. That just… wasn't her usual style. Every time she'd left after a night of sex it had been from the home of someone she'd been dating. Not that she'd had a boyfriend in a few years. Work had just become too overwhelming. She would never regret that cost, not now when she had a dream job. She was head of Public Relations for a well-respected and powerful charity, one that not only did a lot of good, but was well-known in the community. Sharon couldn't deny that it was a great step for her personal career in PR, but it was more than that. Now, she could finally help people the way that she had always wanted—by getting the word out and letting potential donors know that even the smallest contribution helped. If everyone contributed five dollars… It was a campaign slogan, yes, but it was also true, and Sharon Talcott was determined to make sure people understood that.

She had big plans for Hearts in Hands. As Ross had mentioned earlier, the charity wasn't very well-known outside its home city of Pittsburgh. There had been talk of perhaps someday moving its headquarters to New York City, where many nationally recognized charities were stationed, but most felt that it was important to keep HiH centered in the city where it had been founded. It was Sharon's job to promote HiH and shape public perception about it, and she was determined that it would one day be as well-known as the March of Dimes or other iconic charities.

Sharon glanced at Ross, who was stretched out next to her. The post-sex discussion had been lively as they'd come down from their high, chatting about the gala and art, but now it had lapsed into a surprisingly comfortable silence. Still, she remembered Ross's stipulation that she should not stay the night. It was probably time for her to shower and then go.

"Mind if I take advantage of your offer to let me use the shower?" She asked, putting that teasing note back in her voice. She'd noticed that he liked it when she had teased him earlier. It hadn't started out as a way to provoke him—only to test the waters. She had been curious to see if he would continue to pursue her if she didn't throw herself at him. Ross had been so open about his intentions, and oddly enough it had made her doubt them. She wondered where he got such confidence.

Sharon had plenty of confidence herself… most of the time. But this job had been touch and go from the start. The last head of PR at Hearts in Hands had left unexpectedly following a family emergency, and she'd had to fill her predecessor's shoes quickly. But the gala had apparently gone well, or had been when she decided to sneak out early with Dr. Tall and Handsome. Even though she had just landed this position and it was her first big event, she still felt guilty for leaving before the party was over. All in all, everyone at HiH seemed to like her.

When it came to love, well, she'd never had any confidence to begin with.

Ross looked over at her, blinking a few times to focus his eyes. Looked like he'd been about to fall asleep, then. But his smile was slow and easy, if a bit distant. "Of course. It's just on the left there. Feel free to grab something from the fridge on your way out if you want, I don't think anything's open at…" He glanced at the clock on the nightstand, "damn, three in the morning."

"Any particular reason you don't want people to stay the night?" Sharon asked before she could stop herself. "I don't mind leaving," she added, backtracking a little. "I'm just curious."

Ross's expression was hard to read in the dark, but she could see him shrug. "I've found that people tend to think a hook-up has some kind of deeper meaning if you let them sleep over."

"I can understand that." Sharon buried her head in the pillow to hide her embarrassment. "I've never done the whole one-night stand thing before, so…"

Ross propped himself up on his elbows and stared at her. "You haven't? Not even when you were young and crazy?"

Sharon laughed. "Not all of us went through a wild phase," she replied, although it wasn't entirely true for her. She had done her fair share of partying with her friend Leticia during college, but when it came to romance she'd always been a traditionalist. "I just always ended up in a relationship instead, so I'm not sure what the proper protocol is."

"Protocol?" Ross laughed. "You make it sound like there are rules for these things. There really aren't. It's just a matter of preference. I don't like it when people stay over, but some people don't mind having overnight guests. Some people love waking up beside their one-night stand and making them breakfast in the morning. It varies."

"I suppose making someone breakfast could be mistaken as proof that you wanted to see them again," Sharon admitted as she thought it over . The way Ross talked about it made her feel terribly naïve. He was so nonchalant, as if he did this sort of thing every night (and for all she knew, he did). But until last night, she had only experienced sex within relationships. She really didn't know how any of this worked.

"Don't look like that," Ross said in a gentler tone. He reached over and tucked a few curls behind her ear, just like he had at the gala. "I didn't mean to be…" He huffed with frustration. "I'm sorry, I'm not good at this."

Sharon pointedly raised an eyebrow and Ross laughed.

"I mean, this talking afterwards thing," he explained. "I just… I had a bad relationship, that's all. Since then I've found it easier, especially with my schedule, to stick to short flings like this. But people seem to get offended by that."

"I don't see that as offensive," Sharon replied. "I mean, my post break-up strategy is usually to cry into a bucket of ice cream, but that's just me."

Ross laughed. "There was a fair bit of that," he replied, winking, and Sharon couldn't tell if he was just joking around or being honest. "It felt like I never did anything right. Nothing was good enough for her. So now I just do one-night stands, and I'm upfront about what I want and what I expect."

"I think that's a fair way to handle things," Sharon replied, "but it does sound a bit lonely."

"Life as a surgeon is lonely," Ross pointed out, lying back on the bed. "I'm constantly being called away, even if it's in the middle of sleep, or lunch, or a birthday party. It doesn't really encourage long-lasting relationships when your girlfriend always feels like they're playing second fiddle to your job."

"I mean, any boyfriend of mine would have to deal with the same thing," Sharon pointed out. "If there's an issue with PR I have to go and deal with it immediately. And I'm seriously unavailable during the Christmas season."

"Date someone who's atheist?"

Sharon laughed and playfully whacked him in the arm. "You know what I mean, everyone uses December as an excuse to go and see family, and I can barely see mine because I'm running from fundraiser to fundraiser. No one's going to want to date a girl who won't put him first."

"I guess this sort of arrangement works for both of us, then," Ross pointed out.

"I'm not sure," Sharon said. "I like the idea of being in a relationship. I mean, my last few haven't worked out, clearly, but I enjoyed the time I was in them and none of them ended horribly."

Ross nodded, and while the darkness made it hard to tell, Sharon thought he looked rather pensive. It seemed that Ross had been in a relationship which *had* ended horribly, and there was little doubt that it had colored his perspective. An experience like that could make anyone afraid to jump into another relationship.

That was a depressing thought.

"Anyway," she said, feeling she had to speak before things got awkward, "I should probably get ready and go."

"Of course." Ross pulled back the covers for her. "Thanks for the night, it was a lot of fun."

'Fun' barely even began to cover it. Sharon knew she was going to be fantasizing about this night for a long time to come. "Same to you, and thanks for the shower."

Sharon untangled herself from the covers and quickly headed to the bathroom. It was a lovely room with a spacious shower. At any other time, she'd take time to relax and revel in the hot spray, but she needed to get out of there as quickly as possible. She didn't want to overstay her welcome. She scrubbed vigorously, trying to ignore how relaxed she felt. Ross had been right about that—she had desperately needed to work out some of her tension.

He'd been right about a lot of things, actually. He'd been right that she liked being praised and told what to do. More importantly, he had seemed to enjoy the fact that she liked her sexual partner to take the lead. In the past, she had been made to feel ridiculous for her submissive tendencies. She had sometimes wondered if she was being selfish by refusing to pull her own weight in bed. It had been nice to sleep with someone who saw her submission as a positive thing.

Sharon stamped down on the warm and fuzzy feeling in her chest. This was a one night stand, one that she'd desperately needed, but that was all. No use in overthinking it… except, perhaps, to keep it in mind for the next time she had a boyfriend. It was a new thing to add to the list of what she needed in a partner. Now that she'd had a taste of what it was like to be dominated in bed without being abused, disrespected, or shamed for her desires, she didn't think she could settle for anything less.

She toweled her hair off as best she could, knowing that her curls were frizzing, and made a note to shower again in the morning with her proper made-for-curls conditioner. As she exited the bathroom, she was stopped short by the sight of Ross lying on the bed.

He'd fallen asleep in the time it had taken her to shower. There was a large window on one side of the apartment and moonlight was streaming in, making his dark hair gleam. Tall, dark, and handsome —it was like he'd wandered out of her fantasies and right into the gala, sporting a fitted suit and that predatory grin that made her shiver.

Sharon gathered up her clothes and refused to look at him any longer. This was a one-night stand. She was not going to linger, mentally or physically.

The moment she got into her car, however (after saying goodbye to Jose, who was finishing up the crossword), she called Leticia. It might have been three in the morning, but it was also a Friday, and that meant her friend wasn't going to be asleep for another hour at least.

Sharon could hear the thumping bass as Leticia answered and knew her friend was, predictably, in a club. Leticia was an art historian who worked for the Carnegie Museum of Art, and was the reason that Sharon knew so much about art. She was also the reason Sharon was able to secure a prestigious art gallery as the venue for her gala. But you would never guess Leticia's credentials if you saw her on the weekend. She still partied like she was in college.

"Hey girl!" Leticia shouted, struggling to be heard over the noise. "What are you still doing up?"

"Do you have a sec?" Sharon asked, climbing into her car. She needed to tell someone about this, and maybe get a metaphorical slap to shake her out of her weird post-coital mood.

"Always." There was the sound of something slamming, and all of the background noise vanished. "I've escaped into the alley. What's up?"

Sharon swallowed. "So I might have... slept with someone."

The pause that followed was so heavy that Sharon could feel it. After a long moment, during which Sharon plugged her phone in and started the car, Leticia spoke. "As in, a one-night stand?"

Sharon nodded, then remembered that Leticia couldn't see her, and said, "Yup."

"Oh my God!" Leticia's voice grew shrill and Sharon was grateful the phone was now hooked up to the car and no longer pressed against her ear. "Sharon! Finally! It helped with the stress, right? I told you it would! Who is it? Did you meet at the gala? Oh my God the gala was tonight, how did that go? Are you finally embracing Georges Braque? He wasn't a coworker, was he? Which dress were you wearing?"

Sharon took a deep breath against the barrage of questions, waited for Leticia to finally run out of things to ask, and then told her about the evening. She told her about how the gala had seemed to go well and everyone had seemed to like it, and then how she had been approached by Ross.

"He was so... refreshingly honest about it. Just, 'hey, let's help each other out, and oh by the way, would you like to have sex?'"

Leticia snorted. "I'm sure he put it better than that."

Sharon swallowed, remembering how Ross had put his arm around her waist, how his fingers had trailed along her jaw, and how he'd murmured quietly into her ear. "Hehe definitely did."

"So you went back to his place?"

Sharon described the rest of the night to her. She even admitted how good it had been to relinquish control and let someone else dominate her.

"I told you!" Leticia sounded as triumphant as if she'd been the one who'd just had sex. "I told you that you were a sub! You just had to embrace it."

Sharon pulled out of her parking spot and began driving home. "Kind of not the point here."

"Then what is the point? You found a gorgeous guy, you had amazing sex, and your first big gig with HiH was a success. It sounds like a good night all around."

"It's just..." Sharon struggled to put her thoughts into words. "He's the most emotionally distant person I've ever been with. I mean, the sex, hell yes. I'm almost worried that he was able to read me so well —I must be more obvious than I thought. But it was different from other times I've had sex. I mean, I was always in a relationship before, so of course it was different. Still, it was like he was holding me at arm's length. There were times when he'd smile and it wouldn't reach his eyes, y'know? And afterward… It's not like he was rude—he even offered for me to raid his fridge if I wanted to. But he was so casual about it, like he'd already dismissed me from his mind. Ugh, I must sound so clingy."

"Was he a jerk about it?"

"No, that's the thing. He was perfectly kind to me the entire time. There was just this distance. Like he wasn't letting himself open up."

Leticia didn't answer, and Sharon glanced down at her phone to make sure it hadn't dropped the connection. As she did so, she realized she was about to miss her turn. Shit.

She turned the wheel, trying to pump the brakes, but it was too late—she could feel the car spinning and skidding on the pavement. Shit, shit, shit. She kept bumping the brakes, trying to straight out, but the car was overcompensating on the turn now, heading straight for—

The left side of the car slammed into a sturdy light post and a mailbox. Sharon could feel the car door crumpling. Something crashed down around her leg and she screamed in pain, feeling like her bone had shattered into a thousand shards of glass.

The airbag deployed, knocking the wind out of her and giving her whiplash as her head tipped forward and then slammed back against the headrest. Pain continued to radiate up her leg and Sharon felt bile surge up her throat. Don't vomit, don't vomit, she thought. Please don't add humiliation to this by vomiting.

"Sharon?" Leticia's voice sounded tinny. The phone must have disconnected from the car. "You okay? It sounded like a crash. Sharon?"

"I'm okay," Sharon croaked, surprised at how rusty and dry her voice sounded. "I took a corner too quickly. I-I think I need you to call 911."

"Where are you?"

"Uh... corner of 5th and Lexington." Sharon tried to move her leg out of its metallic vice and gasped. It was like somebody had dipped her leg in molten lava. "I... I think s-something happened to my leg."

"Just hang tight hon. I'm going to call them right now. I'll put you on hold, just hang in there."

The pain was making her vision go white at the edges. Sharon tried speaking again, but it only came out as a murmur. "I think..." The pain was so immense. She couldn't think, couldn't speak, it was all just pain...

Fuzzy blackness closed in around her and then she felt nothing at all.

3

Ross's eyes flew open as his pager started beeping. Back in his medical school days he'd be groggy when he first opened his eyes, but after so many years in the field, his brain had learned to respond instantly to the distinctive beep. He went from a deep sleep to awake and alert in less than a second.

He threw on his clothes and booked it to the hospital. "Shattered leg," one of the nurses told him as he strode in. "Dr. Lahiri said it was best that you operate."

"How'd it happen?"

"Took a corner too quickly, or at least that's what her friend told us. She was on the phone when it happened. The friend was the one who called 911. She said that sometime during the call, the woman passed out."

"From the pain?"

"It seems so. No concussion that we can detect. There's some slight bruising here and there but it seems most of the damage is in the leg."

Ross grabbed some gloves. "All right, bring me to her."

The operation wasn't an easy one. Sure enough, the woman was mostly undamaged, but the leg had really taken a beating. It seemed that the car had hit a light post and a mail box, and so all of the damage had been concentrated in the front left of the car—where the woman's leg was. Luckily, she was under the entire time, so she didn't have to feel anything.

The invasive nature of surgery had always interested him. It was a surgeon's job to get under a patient's skin, to change them for the better, to touch their heart—sometimes literally. Emotions—especially love—were like invisible forms of surgery, working their way through someone's core and leaving them changed. Sometimes, when he was feeling particularly whimsical, he wondered whether those invasive emotions left marks upon the soul, like old surgical scars. But perhaps that was stretching the analogy too far.

In the end, he had to put a rod in the woman's leg. He winced inwardly as he thought of the massive hospital bill she'd be stuck with, not to mention the extensive physical therapy she'd have to undergo. He'd had patients who cried when they awakened to find themselves post-op, because they had no idea how they were going to pay for the expense. He hoped that this woman would be able to afford it.

He sent her into post-op, washed his hands, checked on some other patients, and then waited until the woman had been assigned a hospital room before he checked on her. He liked to have a post-op chat with all his patients. As the person who operated on them, he felt he was best able to explain the operation and answer their questions.

And so it was with a rush of guilt that he opened the door and found himself staring into very familiar blue-green eyes.

"Sharon."

"Ross." Sharon seemed at just as much of a loss as he was, but at least she had an excuse—she'd been unconscious for the surgery. He hadn't. How had he not recognized her?

He knew that he tended to get into the zone, so to speak, when performing surgery, but it worried him that he hadn't taken the time to notice the patient's face. He'd have to do better.

Although, considering their relationship, maybe it was a good thing he hadn't recognized her at the time. No matter how you tried to avoid it, sex was a kind of intimacy—the only intimacy he allowed himself nowadays—and as a doctor he wasn't allowed to operate on someone he had a personal connection to, even if he was the best person for the job.

Seeing that Sharon was still looking at him with confusion and a good bit of hesitation, Ross forced himself to focus on the present moment. "I'm sorry if I startled you. I was the one who operated on your leg."

"Thank you." Sharon sounded genuinely grateful. "I feel so stupid. I ran into a mailbox of all things."

"I think it was probably the light post that did most of the damage," he pointed out. "Don't worry about it. I'm just glad you didn't run into a building."

"I shouldn't have been talking to Leticia. I was distracted."

"The EMTs told me you passed out, so I'm glad you were talking to her. You wouldn't have been able to call 911."

Sharon shook her head, her mouth twisting up into a rueful smile. "I still feel stupid."

It seemed that Sharon's self-deprecation was coming into play. Ross tactfully changed the subject. "Did the nurse explain everything to you?"

"That I have a rod in my leg and I'm going to have to go to therapy? Yeah." Sharon nodded. "I don't think it'll interfere with my work, thank God. I have to keep on top of things, but I can do most of my work from home. Making calls, that kind of thing. I can even have Charlene stop by the apartment to help me out." Continuing on from Ross's blank look, Sharon explained, "She's my assistant. She worked under Liza too—my predecessor—so she knows the ropes almost better than I do."

It made warmth bloom in Ross's chest to know that Sharon's main concern was Hearts in Hands. "HiH seems to be in good hands. No pun intended."

Sharon chuckled. "I just try to do my best. My parents taught me that charity isn't just for the rich. If everyone gives a little bit, they can have just as big of an impact as a few wealthy donors, if not more. Not that we shouldn't shake the rich down a little. God knows they can afford to donate a few thousand. But I want everyone in the city to know about HiH. I want them to make a tradition of donating. Five dollars from every person... Do you know how many people live in the city?"

Ross felt his face hurting and realized that he was beaming at her. Sharon seemed to realize that she was rambling because she blushed, glancing down at her hands. "Sorry. You must think I'm ridiculous, caring more about my job than about nearly losing my leg."

"I think it's noble of you." Ross forced himself to pull the corners of his mouth in and maintain a more neutral expression. "The physical therapy will be hard, and you'll be hyperaware of the rod at times. I have to be honest with you, it won't be easy."

"Do you think it will affect me in the long run?"

"I shouldn't think so. You just have to make sure that your leg is healing properly. The rod will feel weird occasionally. For instance, when you're outside during winter, the rod will get cold, just like any other metal object. You're lucky, though. You're healthy and still relatively young."

Sharon pressed her lips together, a determined light in her eyes. It was similar to the teasing light that had flared in them last night, but it was harder, surer. She might have been tentative in the bedroom, but when it came to her job and her healing, it seemed that Sharon Talcott was not one to be messed with.

"Then I'll just have to keep at it, won't I?" Sharon's tone was light, but that look was still in her eyes. "I'm not going to let this get the best of me. How soon can I start therapy?"

Ross had to work hard to hold in his grin at her determination. "You'll need to be on bedrest for a week so we can monitor you. We need to make sure nothing's wrong, and that everything's starting to knit together the way it should. After that, you can start right away."

"Thank you, again. I know you were just doing your job but it's not an easy one. I mean, 100 years ago you'd have cut my leg off. So thank you."

"I'm just glad you're okay." Ross realized that sounded a little too intimate, and quickly backpedaled. "I, uh, I'm always glad when my patients turn out okay. No matter how hard you try, sometimes there are things you can't save."

"Of course. And thank you." Sharon reached out her hand and Ross took it, not even thinking about it. She gave his hand a squeeze. It was nothing, just a little gesture of gratitude, but Ross felt his face growing hot. What was he, twelve?

Sharon seemed to realize the potential awkwardness of the gesture and withdrew her hand. "You must have a lot of other patients to get to, so I shouldn't keep you."

"It's my pleasure," Ross said, realizing as he spoke that it was true. He was happy to see her again. He was even feeling a little bad for just falling asleep on her and not giving her a proper goodbye last night. "I'll be sure to keep checking up on you."

"Then I look forward to your visits." Sharon's voice was light and even, no trace of innuendo, but Ross couldn't help but imagine certain unethical scenarios all the same.

They would have to be careful of her leg, of course. She couldn't be on top for a while. But if he had her, say, on his kitchen counter, or another surface she could sit on where her leg wouldn't get jostled too much...

He snapped himself out of those thoughts. Sharon was his patient now. Even if he could maintain a sexual relationship with her without inconvenient feelings intruding on either side, he couldn't have sex with her now that she was in his medical care. It would be a huge violation of both his license and his own ethical code.

"Right, then." Ross hoped he didn't sound as awkward as he felt.

"I'll leave you to it. I'm sure you have family and friends visiting soon. Have a great day."

"You too." He might have been imagining it, but he thought he saw some of the light die in her eyes. She almost looked disappointed by his departure.

But that had to be wishful thinking on his part. Something about Sharon made him feel warm inside, and he had to get rid of it before it became something to worry about. "I'll check in on you later."

"See you then!" Sharon waved to him as he walked out the door.

He had better be careful. No matter how sweet Sharon seemed, he couldn't afford to get hurt again.

4

"No way."

"Yes way." Sharon poured a drink of water for herself and for Leticia. "Same guy."

"What are the chances of that?" Leticia said with a grin, folding her arms and sinking down into Sharon's couch.

Sharon had been discharged from the hospital that morning, and Leticia had taken the day off work to pick her up and bring her home. Her leg didn't hurt, exactly, at least not most of the time, but it felt… odd. She was acutely aware that there was something different now, and there were times when she swore she could feel the rod inside of her.

She told herself that she'd get used to it. Just like she'd gotten used to college, and her new job, she would get used to this. It was just a matter of time.

After they had reached the apartment and Sharon had insisted on getting the water herself, crutches be damned, she had told Leticia that the Dr. Hardwick who had operated on her was none other than Ross, her fantastic one-night stand.

"I'm serious," Leticia said, "What are the odds of that?" She pulled out her phone and checked something. "Yup, Google says that there are twelve hospitals in Pittsburgh, although a couple of them look like they're divided into various sub-sections or something like that. Okay, so let's say there are... however many surgeons per hospital..."

"Please don't turn this into a math equation," Sharon groaned.

"I'm just saying," Leticia pointed out, "the probability of your surgeon turning out to be the same stranger you slept with the night before has got to be infinitesimal."

"It was a little weird for me. I think he was fine, though. He seemed fine."

Ross had seemed the picture of calm and support, but in a detached doctor way. The way that he should be, of course, with a patient. Sharon couldn't help wondering what had been going on in his head during their conversation. Had he felt awkward? Guilty? Confused? Did he look forward to helping her, or was he wishing that she was somebody else's patient?

"I don't think you should worry about it," Leticia said. She accepted the water glasses from Sharon, and then watched her critically as she hobbled to the couch. "You sure you got this?"

"I'm going to be working on this leg for a month at least, I need to get used to it. You know I hate being dependent on someone else."

"Unless you're in bed with them." Leticia waggled her eyebrows and grinned wickedly.

Sharon glared at her. "Stop that."

"What? Stop bringing up the fact that you finally had a tawdry one-night stand *and* admitted that you like being dominated in bed? Never."

Something of Sharon's insecurity must have shown on her face, because Leticia immediately sobered up. "Sweetheart, don't worry about it. You said he was professional and he certainly fixed your leg up right. It doesn't have to be awkward unless you make it so. You two had fun, but now you can move forward and maintain a friendly distance, just as if you were coworkers."

Sharon shuddered. Having to work every day with someone she'd once slept with sounded unbearably awkward. Still, there was nothing to be done about Ross now. She would just be polite and friendly, like Leticia said, and it would all be fine. Besides, she wouldn't even have to see him that much. He was her surgeon, of course, but she would see more of her physical therapist in the weeks ahead.

"I hate to change the subject to something more serious," Leticia said, tucking a strand of dark hair behind her ear, "But are you okay with finances?"

That hadn't even been a thought in her head until that moment. "Uh…" Was she okay with finances? Sure, the job at Hearts in Hands was new, so her health insurance might be a bit annoying to sort out but she was sure she was covered. Or was she, since technically she was at fault?

Leticia sighed. "Here, show me the bill. It can't be that bad."

"Oh yes it can," Sharon replied a little more sharply than she'd meant to. "Sorry, sorry. I didn't mean to snap. It's just…"

"I know." Leticia put a soothing hand on Sharon's shoulder.

Leticia and Sharon had met in college, but they'd both come from low income families. Leticia's parents had crossed the border from Mexico and started their new lives in the United States with nothing but the clothes on their backs, and Sharon's mother had squandered all her father's earnings on alcohol. Neither Leticia nor Sharon had needed to panic about bills for a couple of years now, but it was still a specter that haunted their thoughts, peering over their shoulders when taxes rolled around and when it looked like Christmas bonuses might not happen.

"I can look at it, if you want," Leticia said. "I'm sure whatever you fear is worse than it actually is."

Sharon nodded, turned to grab her purse—and realized something. "I haven't been sent the bill."

"What?"

She thought back. They must have sent it to her. She'd been in the hospital for a week, there was plenty of time for them to bill her. They should have at least spoken to her about it, but she couldn't remember anyone mentioning it. That didn't seem right.

"They didn't bill me."

Leticia's eyebrows climbed up into her hairline. "Well, call them!"

Sharon gestured vaguely in the direction of her purse, and Leticia clambered over the couch to pass it to her. Sharon rifled through it until she found her phone. She dialed, followed the automated instructions to reach the correct department, and then waited until the receptionist answered.

"Hello, this is the Billing Department, Miranda speaking."

"Hi, Miranda." Sharon forced a smile into her voice. "I'm sorry to bother you, but I'm a recently discharged patient from the hospital and I was wondering why I hadn't been billed yet for my operation."

"Can I get your name?"

"Sharon Talcott."

"Date of birth?"

Sharon rattled it off, then waited as the receptionist typed in the information.

"You had surgery for your leg, is that correct?"

"Yes, from a car crash."

"Well, ma'am, it says here that your bill has already been paid."

Sharon sat straight up. "What?"

Leticia leaned forward, concerned. Sharon could hardly breathe. Her bill had been paid? By whom? And why?

"Yes, ma'am. It says that your bill was paid in full yesterday by Dr. Hardwick."

Sharon felt a little dizzy, despite the fact that she was already sitting down. "Th-thank you."

"You're welcome, ma'am, have a nice day."

Sharon hung up, still feeling a bit like she was swimming through thick soup. Ross had paid for her operation? But why?

"Sharon? Honey?" Leticia took the phone from her and set it down, placing her hands on Sharon's face to force her to look over at her friend. "Are you okay? What's wrong? Is it more than you thought?"

"It's been paid for." Her voice sounded faint and distant to her own ears. "Ross, the—my doctor, my—he paid for everything."

"Your one-night stand paid for your entire hospital bill?" Leticia leaned back. "Thank God, I thought it was something serious!"

"It is serious, Leticia, I owe him immensely for this!" Sharon tried to keep the panic out of her voice, but she didn't think she'd quite succeeded.

"Hold on now, this is a positive thing. It means that he cares about you, doesn't it?"

"Enough to pay my bill? It can't have been a small amount of money. This isn't like paying for dinner, this is huge."

"Hold on." Leticia picked up her own phone and quickly typed something into it. A moment later she snorted and flipped it around for Sharon to see. "Look, this guy's practically a celebrity in the surgery world."

Sharon took the phone from her friend. Sure enough, there were articles about Dr. Ross Hardwick, saying things like "miracle worker," "groundbreaking," and even, "the real-life Dr. Strange." Minus the magic and arrogance, of course, Sharon thought to herself. And to think, this guy was a huge patron of Hearts in Hands, and she'd had no idea who he was. As head of PR, she should have been familiar with the names and faces of HiH's top donors. As soon as she got back to work, she would need to develop a personal relationship with each of them.

Well, maybe not as personal as the one she had with Ross.

"This guy gives lectures, consultations, I mean look at it," Leticia said, gesturing emphatically at the phone. "Big wigs consistently demand his services for routine surgeries. This guy is rolling in it.

He can afford to pay your bills. It's probably not even a big deal to him at this point, what with his salary."

Sharon handed the phone back. "I still don't know. It makes me feel beholden to him."

"Well, he has to check up on you, right? Talk to him about it."

"I don't know," she says again. Maybe she was just making a mountain out of a molehill, as her dad always used to say.

"Don't do that, Sharon, don't get all up inside your head there." Leticia wagged her finger. "If it makes you feel uncomfortable, then you have every right to tell him so, okay? But personally, I see this as a sign that he cares about you. None of my hookups ever made me breakfast, never mind paid my hospital bill. He sounds like he could be someone special."

"Yeah. Maybe." If she could ever get past that strange aloofness... maybe.

It was such a large and caring gesture, and so at odds with the emotional detachment Ross had displayed after sleeping with her. He had been sexually open, yes, but emotionally closed off. How could such a cold person do something as unexpectedly thoughtful as this?

Sharon didn't know what to think, but Leticia was right—she had to talk to Ross.

5

It didn't take much effort to find out which physical therapist was working with Sharon—generally he directed all his patients to Dr. Chavez, although occasionally the patient's insurance paired them with someone different. Since Ross had paid Sharon's hospital bill, that wasn't an issue.

He told himself that stopping by to see Sharon during her session wasn't a sign that he liked her. He was just concerned for his patient, that was all. It had nothing to do with how attracted he still was to her. Or how determined she'd been after the surgery. Or how much she cared about her job and the cause. He was just being a conscientious doctor.

So why did it feel like he was lying to himself?

Ross pulled up to the physical therapist's office and let himself in. The receptionist, Nancy, nodded at him as he passed. He often came by to consult with Dr. Chavez about a patient, and sometimes to observe the patient's session if Dr. Chavez felt there was something he needed to see *in action*, so to speak.

But this was the first time he'd dropped by unannounced.

He found Sharon in the main exercise room along with a couple of other patients. She was re-training her leg to take her body weight, walking painfully slowly with her hands braced on a pair of handrails. Her face was screwed up in concentration. Ross had a feeling she'd hit him for saying it out loud, but she looked adorable.

Dr. Chavez left the patient he was attending and approached Ross. "This is a pleasant surprise," he said, his Indian accent soft and lilting. Dr. Chavez always spoke softly and calmly, no matter how difficult his patients were. Frustrated with their lack of progress and the pain they experienced, patients often took their anger and fear out on their therapist. Yet Ross had yet to see Dr. Chavez raise his voice or lose his patience.

"I wanted to check in on a patient—Sharon Talcott."

"Ah." Dr. Chavez indicated Sharon with a jerk of his chin. "She's a trooper, that one. She comes in as often as she can and never complains. I wish all of my patients were like her."

"Do you think she'll have a speedy recovery?"

Dr. Chavez thought for a moment. "I have found that half of recovery is belief. The patient who truly believes that they will get better, and does not let setbacks discourage them, recovers faster than the patient who allows their fear to rule them. So far, Ms. Talcott has shown great belief in her own recovery. She has already made great strides, and I think, with her attitude, that she will recover quite rapidly."

"Good." The news made Ross feel warm inside again, but he did his best to ignore the sensation. "Mind if I stop and say hello?"

"Not at all. She's gotten used to the routine, so I let her do it on her own. If you notice anything amiss, please call me."

"Of course."

Leaving Dr. Chavez to his other patients, Ross crossed the room to Sharon. She was so wrapped up in her exercises that it took her a moment to notice him. She really was adorable.

"Fancy meeting you here," Ross joked.

Sharon startled, her eyes flying up to meet his. "Ross!"

He grinned helplessly. Damn it, what was this woman doing to him? "I wanted to check in and see how my favorite patient was doing."

Sharon arched an eyebrow, and Ross had a sudden feeling that he now knew what it was like to be an incompetent underling. "I'm your favorite then? Is that why you paid for my hospital bill?"

Ah, he was wondering when she'd notice that. Truth be told, he didn't quite know why he'd done it. "Concern for his patient" didn't quite cover it. Perhaps it was just guilt-she'd been on her way home from his apartment, after all, and she'd been running on no sleep. If he hadn't kicked her out, she could have gotten some sleep and headed home well-rested. And it wasn't like he couldn't afford it. He'd paid off his loans from medical school long ago, and since then he'd had nothing to spend his money on except for himself and his charities. It felt nice to spend the money on someone else, someone who needed it and could appreciate it. Not that he didn't feel good donating to charities, but he rarely got to see the direct results of his donations. This felt different. More personal.

Ross realized that he actually liked the idea of taking care of someone.

Sharon, however, did not look especially pleased. She didn't look angry so much as upset. "I wish you hadn't done that."

"Why not? If you're worrying that I can't afford it, don't."

"I'm head of PR for HiH, so part of my job is knowing who our biggest donors are so I can hit them up for more cash. I know what you can afford." Sharon took another step, wincing as she put her weight on her bad leg. Ross reached out a hand, but she waved him off. "You're going to think I sound silly, but I don't feel comfortable with you paying for my bills and it has nothing to do with whether you can afford it or not."

"Then why is it?"

Sharon stopped walking and leaned against the handrails. "Ross, I barely know you. We slept together once, and then by sheer coincidence you were my surgeon. Don't you think it's a little presumptuous of you to pay my bills for me? I mean, even if you were my boyfriend I'd feel a little uncomfortable with it. But you didn't even ask my permission. Am I supposed to feel beholden to you now? In your debt?"

When she put it that way, Ross could see how his gesture might have been misconstrued. "I'm sorry. I didn't realize I was crossing a boundary. I felt..."

What he wanted to say was "I felt like I should take care of you," but not only did he suspect Sharon would find a way to kick his ass for it, bad leg or no, but he himself didn't know what to think of that sentence. He owed this woman nothing. He barely knew her, as

Sharon had just pointed out. Why would he feel a responsibility towards her?

He remembered how she'd been when they had slept together—how she had followed his every order, trusted him, even goaded him into taking control when he hesitated. He didn't want to control her outside of the bedroom, but he liked the idea of her continuing to trust him. He wanted her to put her faith in him and his ability to make her happy.

Dear God, what was this woman doing to him?

Ross realized that he'd stopped talking and that Sharon was still staring at him expectantly. He cleared his throat. "I, I felt a bit... guilty. I didn't even say goodbye to you before you left, and then you got into a car crash. I should have let you stay the night and get some sleep."

"If I'd been too tired, I would have said so." Sharon's expression softened. "It was my talking on the phone and being distracted that landed me here, Ross, not you. I promise."

Ross nodded. "But now I do have reason to apologize. I crossed a boundary. Let me make it up to you."

"Oh?" That teasing light came into Sharon's eyes again. "And how do you plan on doing that?"

"By taking you out to dinner, if you're up to it."

Wait, why had he said that?

Sharon seemed as taken aback by his suggestion as he was. "I..." She licked her lips, and Ross's eyes tracked the movement. He wanted to get his hands on her again. He wanted to kiss her breathless and make her cry out like she had the other night. He wanted to feel her thighs trembling under his hands again. He wanted to feel her tight, wet heat around him...

Ross clenched his hands into fists at his sides. He was not going to get an inappropriate boner in the office of his colleague and friend. Hell no.

Maybe he was crazy, but he could have sworn that he saw answering heat in Sharon's eyes. She was blushing slightly, just as she had at the gala, and her eyes darkened. She still wanted him too, didn't she? He wasn't reading this wrong, was he?

Sharon glanced down at the ground. When she spoke, her voice sounded like it had when they'd first met at the gala: pitched up and forcibly even. "I don't think that would be a good idea, Ross."

"No, of course, you're right." She was his patient now. Dating her could get him into serious hot water. Yet... he still felt disappointed.

Sharon looked up at him, and surely he wasn’t imagining the disappointment etched into her features. "I should get back to my work."

"Right, of course. Do you need any help?" He desperately wanted to assist her in some way. In any way.

"I can manage, but thank you." Sharon turned and resumed her slow walking, a polite but clear dismissal.

Ross nodded, feeling awkward, and then he left. He felt an odd aching feeling in his chest, and his thoughts were a jumble. Why had he asked her out? And why had he felt so disappointed when she had turned him down?

He had to get Sharon Talcott out of his system. This was getting dangerous.

6

Dammit, why did Ross Hardwick have to show up at her therapy session?

Sharon thumped the kitchen counter in frustration. She'd been doing such a good job of forgetting about him. Okay, yes, so she might have gotten herself off to thoughts of him once... twice... a few times over the last couple of weeks. She couldn't help it. His low, velvety voice, his mischievous grin, and his large, soft eyes haunted her.

Damn the man. Damn him for being handsome, and rich, and smart, and paying her bills and then apologizing for it, and then asking her out to dinner… What the hell had that been about, anyway? He'd made it very clear to her that he wasn't interested in dating. She had known that about him before she'd known anything else, because it was one of the first things he'd mentioned at the gala. Why would he be asking her out now?

She had to get him out of her head. Normally she'd call Leticia and they'd have a night on the town, but thanks to her leg, that wasn't going to happen any time soon. And she wasn't the type to just go to a bar and pick someone up. As Leticia had been happy to point out, Sharon didn't do one-night stands. Except with Ross, apparently. And now that one exception was reminding her of why it was a rule.

Her phone beeped and she picked it up, checking her email. Working from home had proved to be even easier than she'd expected. Her work mostly involved phone calls, and when she needed to meet with a potential donor or colleague in person, she just sent Charlene in her place. It had all been going smoothly.

This email wasn't about work, though. It was from the hospital.

"A post-surgery check-up?" Sharon said it out loud, just to make sure it was real. She had to go in and see Ross?

She wasn't sure she could handle it.

But the email was very specific, and she knew that it was the right thing to do for her leg. The appointment, the email explained, would probably involve an x-ray to ensure that her leg was healing properly and that her body was accepting the rod. It was just an annoying coincidence that it would require her to see the man she was trying to avoid thinking about.

Why did the universe do this to her? What had she done to deserve this?

"I must have been very bad in a past life," she muttered to her coffee maker.

The coffee maker, although excellent at dispensing liquid caffeine, had no advice to offer.

The next day, Sharon asked Charlene to drive her to the hospital. "I feel bad," she confessed. "This can't be in your job description."

"Don't worry about it." Charlene flashed a grin. The girl was tall and lanky, with light blonde hair and blue eyes, but she still managed to remind Sharon of Leticia. They both had the same way of smiling easily, and both seemed to have boundless energy. "It's no problem."

Charlene dropped her off at the front entrance. "I'll park the car and wait for you in the lobby."

"Thanks again," Sharon said.

"And again, don't worry about it!" Charlene flashed her another grin and then drove off into the parking structure.

Sharon turned to face the hospital entrance, leaning on her crutches. Well, there was no sense in delaying the inevitable. She had to face Ross sooner or later, so it might as well be sooner.

She checked herself in and was initially assessed by a nurse, so she began to hope that maybe she wouldn't have to see Ross after all. This hope was dashed when the nurse left her in an examination room, telling her that, "Dr. Hardwick will see you in just a moment."

Sharon waited nervously, reading the posters on the walls over and over again until she thought she might have them memorized. Just when she thought she was going to scream from anticipation, the door opened and Ross entered.

She had tried so hard to think of him as Dr. Hardwick in her head. She had tried to tamp down on her attraction to him. But now that he was in the room with her, his dark gaze so heavy on her that she could almost physically feel it, it was all she could do not to beg him to kiss her.

"Nice to see you again, Sharon," Ross said. He sounded amicable but distant. It was hard to remember that this was the same man that had paid her medical bills and then asked her out on a date just a few days ago.

Ross looked at her chart. "You seem to be recovering well. Any unusual pain?"

Sharon shook her head. "I mean, there's discomfort sometimes, but it seems like that's normal. From what the nurse told me."

"Unfortunately, yes." Ross grimaced. "It's what happens when you've got foreign objects in your body. Is it just the rod, or are the screws in your ankle giving you issues? Most people experience discomfort with either one or the other, and it's usually the screws because your ankle is where most of your mobility is."

Sharon had to hold in her sigh of frustration—her mother had always said she was an impatient one, and this was definitely proving that. "How long will my recovery take?"

Ross gave her a stern look, and Sharon knew instinctively that he had given many a patient that look over the years. It really shouldn't be turning her on, or reminding her of how he'd taken control, and how she *wanted* him to take control and force her to obey his every instruction.

Bad Sharon, she thought. You're in a goddamn hospital!

"It might take up to a year to get your leg completely back to the way it was," Ross said, setting down his clipboard, "And even then there might be permanent changes. Your leg might shrink a little, for instance. That's what the physical therapy is for, to prevent those natural changes from affecting your daily life or changing how you use your body."

When he talked about how she used her body, he was probably just referring to things like walking or climbing stairs. He wasn't talking about… anything else. He couldn't be. But Sharon's mind couldn't help but go there anyway, thinking of Ross being careful of her leg while laying her down on the bed or while spreading her thighs open for him—

Ross crossed the room to stand in front of her, and Sharon was sure that he could hear her heart beating wildly. "Mind if I take a look?"

Her throat was suddenly dry. Not trusting her voice, she just nodded. This was the first time they'd been this close since the first night. She could smell him, a dark, woodsy scent, and with it came all the sense memories of that night together. His hands on her. His mouth on her breasts, her stomach, in between her legs...

It could have been her imagination, but she thought she heard Ross suck in a breath. Could he tell what she was thinking?

He put his hands on her leg, gently feeling along it and testing it for problems. "How does that feel?" He asked, his voice low and rough.

She wanted his hands to roam higher, to pin her down like they had before. Sharon swallowed. "It—it feels fine. No pain."

Ross looked up at her, and Sharon felt painfully embarrassed. Her pathetic arousal must show all over her face, and here was Ross just trying to do his job.

"You sure?" He asked, his voice getting even lower. "You sound... breathless."

One of his hands slid farther up her leg, just to the hem of the hospital gown they'd had her put on. Oh, God, she was wearing nothing but a flimsy paper hospital gown. It would be so easy for him to rip it off of her, leaving her exposed and open to whatever he wanted...

Ross tilted his head a little closer. His pupils were so wide, they made his eyes look black. "Sharon." His voice was nothing more than a rough murmur. "I need you to tell me to stop."

"Why?" Her voice didn't sound like her own. It was too breathy and desperate.

"Because if you don't, I might do something very bad."

With a boldness that came from who knew where, she grabbed his hand and pushed it underneath her hospital gown, right up to where she was starting to get wet. "Does it feel like I want you to stop?"

Ross's eyes darkened even further. A voracious grin flashed across his face, and then he lunged forward, pressing their mouths together and swiping his tongue across her lips. Sharon pressed herself forward as best she could with her bad leg, grabbing frantically at his coat and trying to work a hand underneath his shirt. Ross' hands were everywhere, sliding underneath her gown and grabbing first her ass, then her breasts. Then he gently twisted one of her nipples, making her gasp into his mouth. His tongue slid into her mouth again and again, and God, she wanted him. She wanted him in her, wanted him everywhere…

"I can't stop thinking about this," Ross admitted. He kissed along her jaw, across her cheeks, and down her neck. Sharon tilted her head back to give him more access.

"Me neither," she replied, finally getting her hands under his shirt so she could gently scrape her nails down his chest. Ross shuddered against her, sucking gently where her shoulder met her neck. Then he straightened up to kiss her properly again. Sharon swallowed a whimper as he dragged her up against his body with one hand and kneaded her breast with the other. She was so wet, it felt like she was going to soak through her gown, and possibly even the paper she was sitting on.

Ross was no better off. She could feel his erection through his pants, pressing up against her leg.

It was like she'd been doused with a bucket of cold water. She was about to have sex with her doctor in his place of work, on an examination table!

Sharon pushed Ross back. "We—we can't."

Ross blinked, his eyes thick with lust. It seemed to take him a minute to process what Sharon had said. She knew the moment he did because his face flooded with guilt.

"You're right." Ross stepped back. "I'm sorry, that was extremely unprofessional. I took advantage—"

"I literally told you to take advantage." Sharon still felt out of breath, and she hated how raw her voice sounded. She must look a complete wreck. "I just... anyone could walk in."

"No, you were right to stop." Ross ran a hand through his hair. "But I do want to keep doing this. If you want."

Sharon didn't know what to think. She wanted Ross. She wanted him so badly that she could literally taste it. But she also had no idea what to expect from him. He had made it clear that he didn't want a romantic relationship, but Sharon didn't know how to settle for anything less.

"I still want to take you out on a date, if you'll let me." Ross sounded incredibly sincere. "Now I owe you two apologies."

"You don't have to apologize for this." Sharon sighed, trying to compose herself.

"Still. Let me take you out. Please."

Ross sounded serious. He even sounded nervous, which somehow made his offer more tempting. Sharon hadn’t previously thought Ross capable of feeling nervous, and that subtle display of vulnerability made him seem more approachable. Going on a date with him was still probably a terrible idea. He could break her heart so very easily. But she wanted him so badly, and he seemed to be in earnest.

Could she risk it?

Sharon took a deep breath. Be positive, she thought. Like Leticia said. This could be a fun way to relax. And if nothing else, she'd get free dinner out of it.

"Sure."

7

Ross triple-checked his reflection in the mirror. He had tried to strike a balance between informal and overdressed, and after agonizing over it for an hour he still wasn't sure he had succeeded. After seeing Sharon's reaction to the fact that he'd payed her bills, and remembering how uncomfortable she'd been at the gala, he had picked a somewhat casual Italian restaurant near his apartment rather than one of the upscale places he usually took people he wanted to impress.

Which worked out just fine, because he wasn't trying to impress Sharon. If he wanted her to see him in a good light, that didn't make her special. He always tried to put his best food forward and come across as the competent, successful man he was. It didn't mean anything.

At some point his denials had become paper thin, but he still made them. It felt like the last defense of a desperate man.

He had chosen a light pink button-down shirt with the sleeves rolled up and his nicest pair of jeans. It had felt like a good compromise at the time, but now he was second guessing himself. Should he have gone with the blue shirt instead?

Ross braced himself against the bathroom counter and took a few deep breaths. It really didn't help that the last time he'd been on a date, he'd still been in a relationship with Amanda. In fact, if he thought about it... yes, his last date had been when he'd taken Amanda to that Thai-Mexican fusion restaurant, the new one that she'd been insisting they try. It had been just two days before...

Before Mom died.

Ross took another deep breath, forcing himself to calm down. This wasn't going to be anything like last time. Sharon wasn't anything like Amanda. He had his priorities straight, and he wasn't going to let anyone mess with his head or control him. He was in control. And besides, this wasn't serious. This was just one date, a way to make up for his blunders.

He still couldn't believe he'd almost fucked Sharon in his examination room. He'd been so close. When she had pushed him away, he'd been about to undo his pants. Not that Sharon needed to know that. His intentions had been incredibly unprofessional and could have gotten both of them in huge trouble. Sharon didn't deserve that. Yes, as she had been quick to point out, she *had* encouraged him, but he had started it. He had touched her first. He had invaded her personal space and made it obvious what he wanted to do to her.

That must be what he was feeling: concern for the future of his career. Sharon was his patient, and he could lose his job if the board took his actions the wrong way. The fact that he'd slept with her before the crash meant he could technically claim a prior relationship, but he knew himself to be on shaky ground.

He was just worried about his career. It had nothing to do with Sharon herself. Nothing to do with the way she teased him. Nothing to do with her beauty, or her stubbornness, or her integrity. It also had nothing to do with Amanda, or his fears, or his heart.

Nothing at all.

8

Sharon tried to remember to breathe as the hostess led them through the restaurant. It was a lovely little Italian place a short distance from Ross's apartment—admittedly not what she had expected him to choose for their date. She had seen the building Ross lived in and the high-end minimalist style of his apartment. She had expected him to take her to someplace much more… she didn't want to say pretentious, but, well… fancy. Someplace fancy.

This looked like the kind of restaurant that Sharon would go to with Leticia or another friend. The casual atmosphere helped somewhat to put her at ease, but she couldn't get the tight knot in her chest to unwind itself. She was on an actual date with Ross. She had never considered that was even a possibility. In her daydreams, it had always been a question of whether she'd give into her desire to sleep with him again. She had never imagined that he would ask her out on a proper date.

At least enough time had passed that now her leg was mostly healed, so she didn't have to hobble through the restaurant drawing looks of sympathy. Now she just limped slightly and wore an ankle brace that most people didn't even notice. Which was good, because she had enough to worry about.

What if she scared him off during the course of the meal? What if he realized that she wasn't as sophisticated or educated as he would expect a romantic partner to be? What if she bored him, or annoyed him, or said the wrong thing? It was so hard for her to read Ross—one minute he was warm and friendly and willing to go out of his way to take care of her. The next, he was being cool and professional. And the next, he was making out with her like he'd die if he didn't touch her again.

But maybe this was just what she needed. This date was her chance to finally spend time with him and actually start getting to know him.

The hostess sat them at a lovely table by the window. "Enjoy your meal!"

Her tone seemed to have genuine warmth in it, which was explained by Ross's next comment. "I used to eat here a lot before work got too overwhelming."

"What would you recommend, then?" Sharon asked. She was burning with curiosity. She wanted to ask Ross about his work, and about what it had been like just starting out. She wanted to follow that little breadcrumb of information until it led to a trail that would take her all the way to the heart of who Ross was.

And man, if she was thinking in fairy tale metaphors, she was definitely nervous.

"The carbonara is great," Ross said, pointing to it on the menu. "I hope you like Italian, I just realized that I didn't ask you before I brought you here."

"I love it." Sharon smiled as his question brought back fond memories. "I don't get to eat it much. I spent school breaks with Leticia's family, so I ate a lot of Mexican food. And growing up I ate way more Hot Pockets than I should have."

"Oh man, same here with the Hot Pockets." Ross laughed. "My mom was always working, so I usually had to fend for myself for dinner. And later when I was in med school, I never had time to cook, so my microwave was my best friend."

"What was it like, going through med school?" Sharon asked. "I just got a bachelor's, I've never experienced anything like that."

"It was intense," Ross acknowledged. "We have high school students who come to visit the hospital to see if they want to be doctors. I always tell them, don't do it unless you really want to. Even setting aside the cost, you're going to spend the next few years not sleeping."

"And why did you really want to?"

Sharon half-expected Ross to dodge the question. It was, after all, a very personal one, and they hadn't even ordered dinner yet. But Ross surprised her. "My dad died when I was about five years old. He was in construction and there was an accident on-site. I grew up fascinated with surgery. Maybe it hadn't saved my dad, but the fact that you could go inside a person's body and fix what was wrong with them? To a kid my age, that was a powerful idea. It was a bit morbid of me, spending so much time thinking about the way that my father had died, but I didn't think of it that way at the time. It was a way to cope with the loss."

“I think all kids are a little morbid,” Sharon commented. She offered him a small, reassuring smile. “Once they understand death, they tend to speak more frankly about it than adults do.”

“Fair point,” Ross replied, relaxing a little. “Lisa, the woman who operated on my dad, would visit my mom all the time when I was little. She felt so bad that she couldn’t save him. It gave me so much respect for her. She saved lives every day, and she developed strong connections to people she hadn’t technically even met. It made me want to save people the way that she did. When I was in high school she moved to England with her husband, but we still talk every once in a while. She always encouraged me to go to medical school, even when my mom was scared about student loans and other school expenses.”

“I can understand that fear,” Sharon said, thinking of her rapid pulse and her sweaty palms when she had learned how much student debt she would have shouldered by the time she finished college. She had only just finished paying off those loans a year ago. “But I’m glad that you persisted.”

“So was Lisa who had the biggest influence on my career choice, with some help from my mom. I can still picture her face on my graduation day. And I know it’s stupid, but every time I help a patient through surgery, I always think of Lisa, because now I understand how she feels. I didn’t always, as a kid. It was so obvious to me that it wasn’t Lisa’s fault and that she’d done everything that she could. My mom never blamed her either. But Lisa had carried that burden on her shoulders, and now that I’m in her shoes, I get it. I want to save every patient that I come across, and when I don’t, it just… it eats at me. I can’t shake the feeling that if I was better, or faster, or *something*, I could have fixed things and they would still be alive.”

"Even on successful surgeries I find myself thinking, maybe if I had done this or that, recovery would be easier for them. Or maybe if we'd been a little faster, I could have prevented this side effect.

"But, it's my job, and I love it, and I wouldn't trade it for anything else. Even if my sleep schedule is completely shot because of it."

The sincere, warm look in his eyes in addition to the words he was saying made Sharon's heart swell. *You're a hero*, she wanted to say. *Also, I'd like to drag you into the bathroom and suck you off right now because apparently being into a selfless hero is a kink I have.*

"You're making me look bad," she joked instead.

"Says the woman who's dedicated her life to promoting a life-saving charity," Ross countered. "What led you into that line of work?"

Sharon tried to stifle her self-conscious laughter. "Growing up, my parents didn't have a lot. Somehow, every year, they managed to scrape some money together to donate to charity. If ever they saw some natural disaster relief fund, they'd immediately send five dollars. I didn't understand it as a kid. We barely had any money of our own, and how could five dollars help anyway? But my parents always told me that if everyone gave five dollars, it would add up quickly. Individuals don't have to give a lot if everyone is giving a little. And they were real believers in that idea of what goes around comes around."

"They sound like good people."

Sharon nodded. "They… they are. They're complicated people. I think everyone is, of course. But most people I know grew up with one of two opinions about their parents; they were either saints or demons. It was never like that for me. Anyway, I spent a lot of school breaks with Leticia's family. But I've started to rebuild my relationship with my parents the last few years. They were a huge influence in my life and I'm glad I still have them around."

Ross nodded in thanks as their server set down their water glasses and introduced herself. When she left, he resumed the conversation. "I understand that. I miss my mom every day, but I'm glad that I had a good relationship with her. I don't regret anything."

"That's wonderful. What was she like?"

Ross was more than ready to launch into a description of his mother, Evelyn, who seemed to have been an absolutely wonderful woman. From there, the meal progressed with an ease that Sharon hadn't expected. She told him stories of her time in college, when Leticia was assigned as her roommate freshman year and subsequently ended up dragging Sharon on adventures all over town. Ross responded with tales from his medical school days, and that led to some gossip about previous coworkers. When their server returned for their dessert orders, Sharon was surprised to discover just how much time had passed.

If she was being honest, she hadn't expected it to go so well. Now she found herself wishing the date didn't have to end. Ross was funny and intelligent, and she just wanted to keep talking with him for hours.

Ross insisted on taking care of the bill— "This is my apology gift, remember?"—and while waiting for their server to return his card, he grew surprisingly shy. If Sharon hadn't seen how sexually confident he was, she would have said that Ross was anxious. "Would you…" he cast his eyes down at the table. "Would you like to come back to the apartment?"

Sharon remembered the way Ross had grabbed her in the examination room and recalled the raw power she'd felt emanating from him with every insistent touch and bruising kiss. She wanted him to do that again, to grab her and pin her against the nearest surface and *claim* her.

But it wasn't just raw desire she was feeling. Now she knew him better on a personal level. She understood him more than she had before their date began. They had spent hours laughing and joking together. It was like a switch had flipped in her head, and she now had permission to admit how much she still wanted him. She crossed her legs, trying to relieve some of the tingling anticipation she could feel building between them. "I—yes, I'd like that."

Ross grinned, his eyes darkening just a bit. Sharon pressed her legs tighter together. "Then why don't we get out of here."

9

There was a different doorman working in the lobby when Ross and Sharon reached his apartment. Ross was a bit glad —he had nothing against Jose, of course, but he didn't want anyone realizing he'd brought the same girl back twice. It had never happened before, and the last thing that he needed was for the staff in his apartment building to start speculating about his love life. He had a reputation as a good guy who happened to have a lot of perfectly polite one-night stands, and he was content to keep it that way.

He briefly wondered if the real reason he was glad for Jose's absence was because he didn't want to admit to anyone, even himself, that Sharon was becoming important to him. He was happy to have an excuse to bury that thought and forget about it, preferably forever.

Sharon gave him one of her coy looks from underneath her lashes as they entered the elevator. "Think you can keep your hands to yourself for thirty seconds, Dr. Hardwick?" She asked.

Oh God, he wanted to devour her right there for that comment. "I think I can manage."

Sharon made sure to walk ahead of him while they were headed down the hallway to his apartment, her ass swaying as she all but strutted. She leaned back against the wall while he unlocked his door, her eyes sultry as she watched him. "What are you thinking about?" He asked. "Tell me." He made sure to put a bit of his growl into his voice.

Judging by Sharon's responding shiver, she'd liked that growl. "I'm thinking about how you grabbed me the last time, how you seemed almost out of control." Ross could see how dark her eyes were becoming and how her chest was fluttering as her breath became shaky. "I was thinking about how I wanted you to do that again."

Ross pushed open his door and stepped back, an invitation for her to step inside. "You want me to do that again?"

Sharon nodded. She seemed to be a bit hesitant.

"You like it when I take control?"

She nodded again. She still didn't step inside. Ross could feel his eyebrows drawing together and his mouth drooping in a frown. "Does that make you uncomfortable?"

Sharon looked away. Her eyes were glassy, like she wasn't really seeing anything in front of her. "I like it, I do. I have to be such a control freak at my job, and growing up with… I was always in fear of slipping up, of falling prey to something and losing my control. And with my job… I just, I have to be in control and I want to be. But it gets so exhausting and so I like… I like that you take that away and I like the idea of just letting you—but it…"

She seemed to be floundering, so Ross took a step closer. "It scares you?"

"Yes."

Ross felt the urge to hug her and had to swallow hard to overcome it. "It's okay. We don't have to do anything you're not comfortable with. You can give up as much or as little control as you want to."

Sharon looked at him, her eyes shining with gratitude. "Thank you."

"Tell me what you want," Ross urged. "Let me know and I'll do it. I want to make sure I'm not crossing any line."

Sharon finally stepped inside the apartment. Ross followed and closed the door behind them. She kept walking, going backwards until she was only a foot in front of the wall next to the doorway that led to his bedroom. "I want you to pin me down and... and fuck me."

Ross advanced on her, just a little. He didn't want to scare her. He could practically see Sharon willingly giving up control, loosening a usually white-knuckled grip. He remembered how tightly she'd held onto her steering wheel, and the whitening of her knuckles as she gripped his bed posts. He wanted her to feel relaxed and to trust him.

"Where and how?" He asked.

Sharon opened her mouth, then closed it again, shaking her head. "I don't know. I want you to decide. Please."

Ross nodded. "Okay then."

He lunged forward, pinning her to the wall. He lifted his hands to brace himself against the wall and bracket her in. "What about..."

He slid one hand down her left thigh and hitched it up around his waist. "Here?"

Sharon's breath caught and Ross bit his lip to try and hide his triumphant grin. He loved how easily he seemed to take her breath away. He felt the creamy skin of her thigh and was immediately grateful that she'd chosen to wear a dress that night. He slid his other hand up her dress, expecting to meet lace, but his fingers kept going and going and he realized—

"You're not wearing underwear."

The grin that Sharon gave him was nothing short of wicked. Her eyes flashed, and Ross couldn't help it—he kissed her, as slowly as he could. And then he kissed her again. And again. He loved that spark of playfulness in her, the way she played coy to prompt him to assert control over her. It helped to reassure him that she truly wanted this, and that she wanted him to take care of her in this way.

Sharon slid her hands underneath his shirt and up his back, her nails scraping lightly as she exposed his skin to the cool air. Ross lifted her leg up even higher around his waist and ground against her, letting her feel how aroused he was. He could certainly feel her. Even through his pants, he could feel the heat of her and the wetness starting to slide down the inside of her thighs. He couldn't wait to be buried inside her.

One of Sharon's hands cupped around the back of his head. She pressed down gently and Ross followed her lead, breaking off the kiss and ducking his head to suck at her throat. He moved his other hand down to grasp the back of the leg that still supported her.

"Ready?" He growled against her throat, pressing the words into her skin.

He could feel her trembling as she nodded, but her arms wound more tightly around him as if to pull him impossibly closer, so he knew it was from arousal and not from fear. Ross braced himself and hefted her up, wrapping both of her legs around his waist. Sharon gave a little squeak but clung to him. She laughed into his mouth as he kissed her again.

"I'm going to have to find a way to pin your hands down like this," he mused, pushing her dress up so he could touch her breasts. "Get you tied up with your legs spread."

Sharon moaned and grinded against him helplessly.

Ross grinned, kissing just underneath her ear. "You like that idea? You want me to tie you up? Leave you at my mercy?"

Sharon gasped in time with her movements and uttered soft sounds of pleasure with every roll of her hips. Ross let her continue as he talked to her. "Who would have thought you liked dirty talk, Miss Talcott? You want me to tell you how it would feel to leave you all strung out and unable to touch yourself, unable to touch me, just having to take everything I give you?"

He bit down lightly on her earlobe and tugged, simultaneously rubbing slow, tight circles around her nipples. "Such a wild thing you are. I bet you could get off just like this, listening to me talk as you fuck yourself against me. I'm almost tempted to let you finish this way."

Sharon whined, her hands wildly grasping at his back and shoulders. "R-Ross," she gasped, the word going up into a high whine at the end. "Please…"

"Please what? Please get inside you? Please let you finish right here, like this?" Ross was careful to keep his voice lazy and detached, as if he was discussing the weather. “It might be nice to slide into you after you’ve already come. Once you’re pliant and relaxed. You’d be so ready for me then, wouldn’t you sweetheart?”

Sharon let out a long, low moan at that, and Ross couldn’t help but chuckle. She was so sexy like this, driven wild and unable to stop herself from grinding against him. His pants were painfully tight, and while he liked the idea of keeping her pinned and letting her use him like this, he couldn’t wait any longer.

“But that’ll have to wait for next time.” Ross moved his hands back down to her legs and hoisted her up just that little bit higher so he could shove his pants down and line himself up. “Would you like to do the honors?” He asked, fishing a condom out of his back pocket before his pants fell down completely.

Sharon’s eyes were glazed and distant, but after a moment she blinked and focused again. She grinned at him, wicked, and plucked the condom from between his fingers.

Ross groaned as Sharon ran her hand over him, pumping him a few times before and after she slid the condom on. The impossible woman couldn’t just get down to business. No, she had to keep teasing him even after he’d seen and felt how desperate she was.

“Let me know if it gets to be too much,” he warned, and then slid inside.

Sharon let out a half-moan, half-sigh of relief. She wrapped her legs around him as tightly as she could before rolling her hips. Ross thrust in and out slowly a couple of times just to make sure she was ready, and then the pace he set was hard and fast—almost brutal.

The scream of *yes* that Sharon let out made him spasm with pleasure. God, she was perfect like this, eager and desperate, letting him pin her to the wall and do as he pleased with her. He was definitely tying her up next time if she'd let him. He'd tie her down and keep her on the edge until she was sobbing and begging. But right now, right *now*, he could only think about how many times he could dive into her clenching, welcoming heat, and the sound of her voice as she screamed his name.

Afterwards, he let Sharon use the bathroom first while he put his clothes in the laundry hamper and threw away the used condom. To his surprise, when she exited the bathroom, she made straight for the door.

Then he remembered his rule. No staying the night.

Ross closed his eyes and took a deep breath. He wanted to keep seeing her. Hell, if he were younger, he would already be dragging her into bed for round two. "Sharon."

She paused, half-turning. "Yeah?"

Ross held out his hand to her, trying to stifle the terrifying emotions rising up in his chest. "C'mere."

Sharon quirked an eyebrow. "You're letting me stay the night?"

"It was rude of me to make you leave before," Ross replied. Sharon put her hand in his and he tugged gently, drawing her close enough wrap an arm around her waist. "Stay."

Sharon looked up at him with an odd light in her eyes. "Okay."

10

Sharon awoke to the feeling of a heavy arm draped over her waist and a warm length pressed against her back. She tried to bury her smile in the pillow, but she wasn't quite sure that she managed it. Ross had asked her to stay the night. She hadn't been expecting that. And he'd been so considerate of her last night. He had made sure she knew he wouldn't do anything she didn't want him to do. She knew it must have been difficult for him. He'd made it clear from their first meeting that he didn't want to date anyone. But perhaps the truth was that he didn't want to *admit* that he wanted to date.

Whatever the case, she wanted to thank him. She didn't know what his work schedule was like, but it was Saturday morning, so she had nowhere to go. Why not thank him properly?

Well, properly in a way that didn't involve more hanky-panky. Although she was happy to do more of that later, she was still a bit sore, and she was sure that Ross was too after literally holding her up last night.

Sharon slowly, carefully, lifted Ross's hand by his wrist and scooted out from underneath him. He made a snorting noise and rolled closer, as if to keep her with him, but she slid off the bed.

Stealing a bathrobe from Ross's closet, Sharon padded into the kitchen. She was glad to see that despite the cliché of male bachelors, Ross actually had a fair amount of food in his fridge. She soon had a couple omelets sizzling away in the pan.

A minute or two after the smell of food filled the room, Ross stumbled in, wearing boxers and a t-shirt and looking—dare she say it—adorable. "You made me breakfast?"

"I wanted to thank you for letting me stay the night," Sharon replied. She slid the omelets onto two plates and sat down, passing one to Ross. "I hope you like them. They're the only breakfast food I'm really good at. My dad used to make everything else."

"Was he a cook?"

"No, I think he just liked it. It was a way that he could spoil us." Sharon thought for a moment if she should reveal any more, but, well, in for a penny in for a pound. "My mom struggled with alcohol addiction, and a lot of my dad's income went straight to the bottle or to her treatment. Rehab was expensive and she was never able to stick to a program. There were a lot of fights, and we didn't really have money because of it, but Dad tried to make us feel special when he could."

Ross stared at her. "And these are the same people that taught you about charity?"

"A person is more than their addiction, although in a way, that's what they become." Sharon sighed, picking at her food. "My parents are good people, but they're complicated, and they made a lot of mistakes. I didn't really have a relationship with them in college, and it took us years after that to mend all the broken bridges."

"But you're in a good place now?"

Sharon nodded, smiling. "Yeah, we're in a good place. My mom's doing a lot better. I'm impressed that their marriage has survived all of this."

"That's true love for you."

"What about your mom?" Sharon asked. "Are you still on good terms with her?"

Ross didn't say anything, but Sharon could see something slide into place in his eyes and his face stiffen a bit. "Yes," he said eventually.

Sharon raised an eyebrow, a technique she'd used many times on irate coworkers. "You know, I can tell when you're lying. You're not very good at it."

"I don't want to talk about it," Ross snapped, like he was some kind of teenager. "Why is that so difficult for you to understand?"

"Excuse me—"

"You just want to know everything and that's… Well, you can't, okay?" Judging by the harsh lines of his face, Ross was angry, but the dark, wet look of his eyes suggested that he was also scared. "I've already shared enough with you."

"You don't have to share anything that you don't want to," Sharon replied, feeling irritation rising. "I just don't want you to lie to me. Say you don't want to talk about it, but don't snap at me when I haven't done anything wrong."

"You keep prying, that's what's wrong," Ross said, his voice rising. "You just need to leave well enough alone."

"I'm not prying, I'm just trying to get to know you."

"Yeah, that's what my last girlfriend said—to me, and to everyone else she was trying to get a scoop from. Worked real well on most people." Ross's tone was cold, almost snide.

Great. What kind of emotional mess had she gotten herself into?

Sharon's mouth tightened. "Well I'm not trying to get a 'scoop,' whatever you mean by that. Share with me or don't, but be honest, and don't compare me to whatever manipulative idiot you got involved with before, okay? I'm not her, and I don't appreciate being associated with her, even if it's just in your own head."

She finished off her omelet and stood up. She didn't need to deal with this. She'd thought that Ross was opening up, and that this could be the start of something more, but it wasn't her job to play therapist. She'd done that kind of emotional labor for previous boyfriends, and it was never worth it.

"I'll see myself out," she told him. She didn't want him to have to worry about exchanging pleasantries.

As she pulled on her dress from the previous night, she decided that sleeping at Ross's place had been a mistake. She should have just gone home. Ross clearly had a lot of boundaries and defenses, and she didn't have the time to knock them all down or navigate them like some kind of minefield.

"Wait, Sharon—"

Ross was suddenly there, catching her wrist as she bent down to grab her purse. She could feel the heat of him radiating behind her, and she knew that if she turned around, he'd be only a breath away from her.

"I'm sorry. This is hard for me to talk about."

She turned to face him, but Ross released her wrist and moved away, scrubbing at his face. "My mom died a few years ago of heart disease. It was… very painful. The doctors did everything they could. I was already successful by then, so I could afford her treatment, but it was torture watching her slowly fade away like that. Sometimes she'd get better and I'd have hope, but then she'd have a close call and I'd lose it again. I can't count how many nights I spent by her bedside in the hospital."

Ross sighed and his shoulders slumped. Sharon thought she could see tears in his eyes. "Being raised by a single mother gave me some advantages. It gave me a huge amount of respect for women, for one thing. But it also meant that she was all that I had in the world. Losing her devastated me."

"I can't even imagine," Sharon said, feeling helpless.

"What was worse was that I was in a relationship at the time." Ross sat down and looked up at her. "I was with the girl that I mentioned. Her name was Amanda. She was the life of every party, the kind of person that you're just drawn to and want to talk to."

Sharon nodded. She knew those kinds of people; Leticia was one of them.

"I thought I was in love with her. Maybe I was. But she was a journalist, and she was all about going to important social events. She wanted me with her to help her get in the door. So while my mom was dying, I kept letting her drag me to these things. The fights we'd have when I didn't agree… She would say that I wasn't supporting her career, but I just… I just wanted to be with my mom…"

Ross cleared his throat, and Sharon knew that she wasn't imagining the tears. "I lost all of my friends because of her. Not that there were any fights, or anything, but they just faded away. None of them liked her. And I couldn't just hang out with Amanda—we always had to be around 'important' people so that she could keep getting information for her stories. She loved scandal and drama. It was her bread and butter, but I just wasn't into it. I wanted a quiet, relaxing life. I thought I was in love with her, and so I just turned a blind eye to all the ways she was hurting me. My mom was dying in a hospital, and Amanda was the only other person I had. Lisa was overseas, I was out of touch with my friends, and so I clung to her.

"Then one night, I was out with Amanda at a social event when I got the call. It was the end. I raced back to the hospital, praying that I'd make it in time. The whole time I kept thinking that I should have been there. I should already have been there."

"Did you make it?" Sharon felt breathless.

He nodded. "Barely. I got about ten minutes with her. Ten minutes to express everything I wanted to say."

Sharon took a tentative step forward. "Would you… would you like a hug?"

Ross blinked up at her, startled, but then he nodded. Sharon pulled him into a hug, letting him rest his head on her shoulder. After a moment, Ross slipped his arms around her waist and held her close.

"I'm so sorry," she whispered. "I can't even imagine how painful that was."

Ross nodded into her shoulder and she tightened her grip. How long they stood like that, she couldn't have said, but she kept holding him until he started to pull away.

"Sorry about that," he said, his eyes downcast.

"Don't apologize." Sharon was surprised at the fierceness in her voice. "You're allowed to mourn. I'm sorry for pushing."

"No, no, I was being a dick about it. I could have been polite in saying I didn't want to talk about it." Ross sighed. "Besides, I wanted to tell you."

"Well I appreciate that you opened up to me and trusted me," Sharon said, trying to convey her earnestness. "You're a good person, Ross. I know that your mom is proud of you."

The corner of Ross's mouth turned up in an almost-smile, and Sharon felt her heart clench. This must be what he was like when he lost a patient, she thought. Maybe not quite this intense, but still. She wanted to be there for that, she realized. She wanted to be the one to hug him, the one to comfort him when he was feeling lost and raw.

Oh no. What had she gotten herself into?

11

Ross pulled up in front of Sharon's apartment and double checked the parking signs. If he got ticketed because he didn't see a street sweeping sign or something of that sort, it wouldn't be the first time. Better safe than sorry. Once satisfied on that point, he threw the car into park and looked up at the building. It wasn't as nice as his, nor was it in such a prime location, but it exuded an air of cozy charm and the surrounding neighborhood looked like a fun place to live.

The moment he stepped into the foyer, he could feel a sense of warmth that was distinctly lacking in his own home. Not that the chilly atmosphere or distinct lack of décor in his apartment was intentional. He wasn't trying to impress anyone with its elegant austerity. It was just that he was so rarely at home due to his work schedule that it seemed pointless to decorate. But this place? This was the kind of setting that made him think of kicking off his shoes and curling up on a comfy couch with a good book. It felt like coming home.

He hesitated in the open doorway of Sharon's apartment, listening to the chatter of several people inside. Last Saturday, after he had told Sharon about his mom (and they had indulged in a round of comfort sex in the shower), Sharon had invited him to come over today. He'd said yes without even thinking about it. He rarely got to spend time with anyone outside of work, and this might be a good change of pace. But now he was second-guessing himself. Was this a little too permanent? Was Sharon starting to think of him as a steady boyfriend?

The idea of being anyone's anything made him want to head for the hills. He'd done that once before, and he could still feel the Amanda's metaphorical claws digging into him. He had been hers, as she'd made it abundantly clear to everyone, and that had meant that his life was supposed to revolve around her. He couldn't do that again.

As he stood there, one foot in and one foot out, Sharon passed by the doorway and saw him. He noticed with pride that she was barely limping anymore. She really had taken to the physical therapy with an intensity and success that he'd rarely seen.

"You came!" Sharon said, waving him inside.

"You sound so surprised," he said.

"I worried that a patient might call you away," she admitted, giving him a hug. Ross instinctively hugged her back, remembering the last time she'd been in his arms, and how he'd been able to just sink into her. He couldn't do that here—her friends would notice—but it was still nice to just hold her for a moment.

"C'mon in, I've got food and drinks out here." Sharon pulled away and gestured at the kitchen island, which was covered in snack foods like queso and chips, salad, chocolate candies, and pigs in a blanket. "Hey everybody, this is Ross. Ross, this is everybody."

'Everybody' seemed to be five people lounging around on the couch and chairs. Sharon introduced them all one by one.

"That's Leticia," Sharon said, gesturing at a pretty Latina woman perched on the arm of the couch. "Watch out, she's never met a stranger.

"That's Jonas," Sharon pointed at a skinny man with dyed purple hair who was in the middle of a tug-of-war for a TV remote with a curvy blonde wearing Star Trek pajamas, "And the nerd he's fighting with is Debbie."

"Takes one to know one," Debbie retorted, which allowed Jonas to gain the advantage and snatch the remote out of her hands. He gave a crow of triumph and flipped the channel from a ballgame to the Food Network.

"And last but of course not least," Sharon finished up, gesturing at the last members of the group, "We have Melanie and Tom. They like to take advantage of the twin thing, ignore it."

Melanie and Tom, a pair of black siblings who were, in fact, wearing identical button-up shirts, gray slacks, and glasses, both raised their right hands and flipped Sharon off while wearing scarily identical grins.

"And that's everybody!" Sharon put her hands on her hips. "Okay, guys, be gentle on this one, he's new."

"I'm always gentle unless someone requests otherwise," Leticia replied with a naughty grin. So this was the famous Leticia. Ross made his way over to her while Sharon went to play referee between

Jonas and Debbie, who were apparently fighting over whether to watch a marathon of Chopped, or Star Trek.

"Ross," he said, holding his hand out for Leticia to shake. "I've heard a lot of good things about you."

"Likewise," Leticia said with a smile that was far too knowing for Ross's liking. Of course, Sharon had every right to talk to her friends about her sex life. He just hoped that Leticia wouldn't read too much into his visit to Sharon's apartment. "So what brings you here tonight, Dr. Hardwick? You don't seem the type to hang out with your one-night stands."

It was a fair question, but it didn't make Ross feel any more at ease. "Sharon and I like each other's company, and she suggested that I might need an evening to relax," he says in as casual a tone as he can muster. "And I could stand to make some more friends, so here I am."

"So here you are." Leticia peered at him through narrowed eyes. "Careful, the queso's spicy."

With that, Ross knew he'd been dismissed—for now, anyway. He wandered over to grab some food and soon found himself wrapped up in a conversation with Tom. It seemed Tom was an artist, and he had heard about Ross's knowledge of Cubism from Sharon.

"I'm lucky that Melanie got a good job and is willing to put up with me," Tom told him, grabbing some glasses from the cupboard and ignored Sharon's fake-annoyed commentary ("Oh no, please, just go through my kitchen Tom—it's not like you left an unholy mess in there last time or anything") as he filled them with water. "I rent out a small studio over in the North Shore neighborhood so I can be near the park and the Warhol museum."

"Have you had any shows recently?" Ross asked.

"Yes, actually." Tom's grin was a bit sly. "You might have seen some of my work at the gala that Hearts in Hands just hosted. Leticia and I worked together to get Sharon the venue for the gala. Leticia works at the Carnegie Museum as an art historian."

"Really?" Ross looked over at Leticia, who was now making commentary on Chopped—it seemed that Jonas had won the television war—and saying something about the time she'd danced topless on top of a bar their junior year of college. "She does not strike me as an art historian."

"Apparently I don't strike people as an artist," Tom replied. "People usually think I'm a lawyer."

"What's it like living with your sister?" Ross asked. "I'm an only child, but I've always wondered what it's like to have siblings."

"There's not really anything like it," Tom said. "I mean, friends come close, but friends are like the positive side of siblings. When you live with someone your entire life and they're your age, you tend to see their bad sides as well as the good. But Melanie and I make it work. We balance each other out. She's a therapist, so in a way, both our careers revolve around emotions. She focuses on the causes of emotions and the best strategies for regulating them in a healthy way, and I'm all about celebrating the chaos."

"Chaos, huh?"

"Life is chaos," Tom pointed out. "You can't help where you end up really. Did you grow up here?"

"Yeah," Ross replied, wondering why he was changing the subject.

"Well, what if you'd grown up in Boston? Or Los Angeles? You had no control over where you started out or where you came from, and you also don't get to dictate how certain things make you feel. At best, you can only control how you react to emotions. You can't control what you're passionate about, or who you fall in love with."

Ross seemed jolted at that last bit. Then a brief moment of what Tom said registered deep down inside. He looked directly at Tom, who was looking at Sharon. Ross got a sick feeling in his stomach. "You're not…"

"Pining for Sharon? God, no." Tom laughed. "I love the girl but not like that. I meant you."

"I'm not… we're friends," Ross finished lamely.

"Right." Tom grinned. "Friends look at each other like that, sure."

Ross looked over at Sharon, who was laughing at something that Melanie had said. As if she could sense his gaze, she turned, still smiling. Ross's breath caught in his throat. He had to swallow hard and force himself to smile back. Sharon looked a little messy. Her hair was pulled back in a sloppy ponytail and she was sprawled inelegantly across the couch, but in that moment, she looked more beautiful than she had when he'd first seen her at the gala.

Then Jonas said something to Sharon and her attention was drawn away. Just like that, Ross felt like he could breathe again.

Tom shook his head, still grinning, and Ross rolled his eyes at him. "We're not dating."

"I never said that you were," Tom replied.

"Stop monopolizing him," Melanie scolded, joining then. "We all want to get to know this Sharon's mystery guy." She turned to Ross with a smile. "Sharon has been refusing to tell us anything about you."

"Don't trust that smile," Tom warned. "She's here to tell you that if you screw Sharon over, she's going to destroy you both emotionally and physically. Like I said she's a therapist—she's good at emotionally destroying people."

"Emotionally destroying people is the *opposite* of my job description. Stop making me sound like an asshole," Melanie said, rolling her eyes at her brother and physically inserting herself between him and Ross. "Now go bother Debbie or something."

Tom held his hands up in a placating gesture, laughing, and obediently went over to join the others.

"I hope he wasn't being painfully obvious," Melanie said, in a tone that implied she had overheard at least part of their conversation. "He just wants Sharon to be happy and he sees how much she likes you."

"Has she really talked about me that much?" Ross asked, taking a sip of water to hide the nervous look he was sure he was wearing.

"No, she's kept things private," Melanie assured him. "But Sharon doesn't do one-night stands, and when she said that she was seeing you again, well… we knew that it meant something. The fact that she invited you here also means something."

"I've been pretty bad about maintaining my friendships," Ross admitted. "I think that was part of it."

"She said that you are a doctor," Melanie replied. "That must take up a lot of your time."

Ross grimaced. "It's not so much that. It's… I lost a lot of friends while I was dating my last girlfriend."

Melanie's mouth pulled into a tight little frown and she folded her arms. "You know that's a sign of a bad relationship, right?" She asked. "If none of your friends like your partner or vice versa…"

"No, I know. She's out of my life."

"Good." Melanie gave a brisk nod. "I just want to be sure that you understand that. Even when someone gets out of a bad relationship, if they don't recognize the things that made it so bad, they're liable to get stuck in a similar relationship again."

Ross couldn't completely hold in his shudder. The idea of being with Amanda, or someone like Amanda, again made him want to throw up.

Melanie's face softened a little. "I'm sorry, it's just habit. As a therapist, I can't really give people answers. I'm supposed to ask questions and help them come to their own answers and conclusions. It's more powerful when you reach the answer yourself instead of having it handed to you. But when I'm off the clock I can do whatever I want, so I sometimes give into the impulse to give advice without thinking."

"No, you're fine," Ross told her. "It's not like you're saying anything that I don't already know."

"Were there other red flags?" Melanie asked. "If you don't mind my asking."

"I don't mind." Something about Melanie's no-nonsense manner made it easy to open up to her. "Um, there were a lot, actually, but I didn't realize them at the time."

"That's how it usually is," Melanie said gently. "It can be hard for us to see the forest for the trees in our relationships."

"That's a good way of putting it," Ross said. "I knew that I was unhappy with her, but I didn't put it all together and realize how selfish and manipulative she was."

He paused as a question came to mind. He glanced at Sharon. She had been light and carefree about their relationship, demanding respect, but never asking for anything more than he was willing to give her. When he looked back at Melanie, she had a soft look in her eyes. Something about her expression reminded him of Tom's sly grin, despite looking nothing like it.

"Is it normal," Ross asked, slowly, "for the memories of a person to still feel… fresh? For you to still have a physical reaction to those memories, even if it's been years?"

Melanie nodded. "It'll happen when you've had an emotionally damaging experience. Even if you don't want to admit it, your body knows it's scared and it'll do whatever it takes to remind you of that feeling so that you don't do it again."

"But I don't want to be reminded. I don't need to be reminded." He didn't want to look at Sharon and think only of Amanda, especially since the two women were nothing alike.

"Have you spoken to anyone about the relationship?" Melanie asked. "And I mean in detail, complete with a good cry?"

"No," Ross admitted.

"I would suggest that, then," Melanie said. "And not as a therapist but as a potential friend. If Sharon has bothered to keep you around long enough to meet us, then you're a good guy, and I'd hate to think that a good guy like you is going around carrying a burden that he doesn't deserve."

Ross didn't know what to say to that. Luckily he was saved from replying by Debbie, who leaned over the back of the couch and said, "Are you two going to keep hogging the food while being all serious, or are you going to bring it over to share with the rest of us like actual human beings?"

Melanie gave Debbie an incredibly fond look, and Ross had to resist the urge to tease her. *Oh, so that's how it is?*

Ross dutifully carried some of the snacks from the kitchen island to the coffee table in front of the couch, and then he followed them up with glasses of water for everyone. Sharon assured him that he needn't go to that effort—her friends were perfectly capable of getting their own water—at which point Debbie piped in to say that the newbie was on the bottom rung of their social ladder and thus had to serve the rest of them.

"I hope you don't treat your paralegal like this," Sharon scolded Debbie as Ross sat joined them, handing Debbie her water glass.

"My paralegal is willing to forgive anything in exchange for designer coffee in the break room and frequent offerings of gourmet cookies," Debbie replied with a grin. "Besides, she already knows she's irreplaceable."

"You're a lawyer?" Ross asked.

Debbie nodded. "I know, I don't look it. Just like Tom doesn't look like an artist in that suit, and Leticia looks nothing like a nerdy art historian. At least Melanie and Jonas look the part, right fashionista?" Debbie poked at Jonas, who stuck his tongue out at her.

"I'm an assistant designer for a niche clothing brand," Jonas explained. "It's a small company, but it's a high-level position, and I'm hoping that I can use the experience to land a job in New York City as a designer or fashion editor."

"He wants to abandon us," Leticia countered.

"Oh c'mon, it's only a…" Jonas grabbed his phone and pulled up a map application. "It's only a six-hour drive! You guys can totally visit all the time. Or just move up there with me."

"For the last time, no, I will not live in that crowded mess of a city," Melanie replied. "And you—" She pointed at Tom, "Don't get any ideas either."

"I take it this is an old argument," Ross said to Debbie.

"As old as time," Debbie said. "Jonas has been threatening to leave us for the city that never sleeps for about five years now."

"As if he could possibly leave us," Sharon said, smiling at Ross over her glass. He knew she was talking about Jonas, but something about the way that she said it while looking at him made him want to reassure her that he, too, wasn't going anywhere—and wasn't that a scary thought.

"But since you've brought up the fact that I'm a lawyer," Debbie said, twisting so that she could look Ross dead in the eye, "Time for the cross-examination."

"Come on, Deb, I didn't invite him so you all could give him an ulcer or something," Sharon said. She then pointed at Ross. "And if you tell me that's not how ulcers work, no more food for you."

"I just have one question," Debbie said. Ross braced himself. "Who's the better captain, Picard or Kirk?"

Ross relaxed. A debate over *Star Trek*, now that he could get into. Satisfied that Debbie wasn't actually going to rake him across the coals, he declared that the calm, even-keeled Picard was the better option, and soon he and Debbie were going at it—she was, apparently, a die-hard fan of Kirk and the original series, despite its cheesy writing.

"Are you kidding me!?" Jonas yelled at the television. "You have only two minutes left, you don't have time to make a vinaigrette!"

"That's the signal, I'm getting the beer out," Tom said, going to the fridge and passing bottles around to everyone.

"He can do it," Debbie said, interrupting her argument with Ross to interject over Jonas's frantic yelling.

Ross, sandwiched between the yelling Jonas and the increasingly-animated Debbie, looked over at Sharon, who just smiled and raised her beer bottle in a silent toast. Ross mirrored both her expression and gesture until Debbie reclaimed his attention to explain the rules of the show.

"Four chefs," Melanie intoned, "Three courses, only one chance to win!"

"Please stop using that voice, it sounds creepy," Tom said.

"Wait," Ross said, hardly able to make himself heard above the chaos. Jonas was swearing loudly because the chef had managed to get his vinaigrette made, but had forgotten one of the basket ingredients, and Leticia was smacking Jonas on the back of the head for swearing. Ross kept talking anyway. "How do you all know each other?"

It made sense for Tom and Leticia to know one another, since one was an art historian and the other an artist. Leticia would have met

Melanie through Tom, and Sharon had been Leticia's roommate in college, so that was where she fit in. But how did Debbie and Jonas meet everyone else?

"Well, Letty and I met each other when I got to be part of an exhibit at the Carnegie," Tom said, "And I met Sharon through her."

"Leticia, Sharon and I all knew each other in college," Debbie said. "I was a political science major before I went to law school. I needed a roommate and so I lived with Leticia, and then we needed a third roommate and got Jonas."

"Letty introduced Tom and Melanie to the rest of us because they were coming over to our apartment all the time," Jonas added. He looked at the television and swore again. "Fuck, c'mon, you don't feed Scott Conant red onions, Jesus. Anyway," he looked back at Ross, "Sharon would come over because it was just where everyone else was, and that was that."

"Although now we're a bit scattered," Melanie added. "Tom and I still have our old place, but Sharon moved to the south side, as you can see, and Debbie, Jonas and Leticia each have their own apartments now."

"I don't see the point of wasting my youth in a courtroom if I can't take advantage of my paycheck," Debbie replied. "And besides, at the end of the day I just don't want to see another human being."

"Says the girl who calls me every night because she's bored and needs to talk to someone about the latest show she's binge watching on Netflix," Melanie pointed out, giving Debbie another fond smile.

Ross wondered, with a funny feeling in his chest, if he wore that same expression when he looked at Sharon. It was worrying how relaxed he felt in this setting, and with these people. They seemed so comfortable around one another, so used to picking up the threads of each other's stories and throwing around playful jabs, and it made him realize how much he'd missed this. He had been out of touch with his friends for so long that he'd forgotten what it was like to be surrounded by this sort of amicable chaos. But by inviting him here today, Sharon had reminded him.

Ross felt his throat tighten in panic. He wanted to run, to get the hell out, to make a dash for the door and run down the steps and get into his car and never look back. Because he was too comfortable here, too open, too vulnerable. The boundaries he'd set for his relationship with Sharon were starting to break down in this atmosphere of zany camaraderie.

But he liked how Jonas was so invested in this cooking competition, and how he seemed to know all the judges' quirks. He liked Debbie's nerdiness, and the fact that Tom and Leticia were now arguing about art ("You can't say that Duchamp's *Fountain* isn't art!" "I will say it as much as I damn well please—"), and how Melanie was giving Debbie a shoulder massage while pretending not to blush. And he especially liked watching Sharon sit on her chair next to the sofa with a beer in hand, quietly watching it all with a soft smile.

And honestly, he deserved to have friends. He deserved to be a little goofy, and hold debates about *Star Trek* captains, and yell at the television about food, and make bets with Melanie about who could shove more chocolate into their mouth. He won that bet, although he nearly choked in the process, which earned him shoulder pats from Sharon while Jonas pointed out how ironic it would be if their group's only doctor needed medical attention. That was when Sharon switched places with Debbie so that she could sit next to him, while Debbie curled up like a cat on the chair and complained about how much food she'd eaten. Meanwhile, Tom, Melanie, and Jonas were a tangle of limbs on the other end of the couch. Leticia was still perched on the arm of the couch as if she hadn't moved all night, and according to Ross's recollection, she hadn't.

Sharon remained pressed against his side, and if Ross worked an arm around her shoulders—and if Leticia raised an eyebrow at him like she could read his mind—what of it? He was three beers in, full of food and M&Ms, with Sharon laughing and smiling up at him, and it felt like all was right in the world for the first time in… well, years.

By the time the night was over, it felt like he had known these people his entire life. It made his chest ache to think of how long it had been since he spent quality time with friends. He should get back in touch with some of his medical school buddies and make more of a point to go out with his coworkers to the local bar. It was unfair both to the people he considered friends and to himself that he wasn't making an effort to spend time with them.

One by one, everyone trickled out of the apartment. Jonas was the first to go, citing some work he'd brought home with him for the weekend that was due Monday. Next was Melanie carrying a food-comatose Debbie, which prompted Leticia to mutter about idiots who needed to get their shit together. Tom left shortly after that, despite having his own transportation, since it was late and the apartment he shared with Melanie was on the other side of town. Soon it was just Leticia and Sharon who were left, and as they chatted quietly on the sofa, Ross took a proper look around the apartment now that it wasn't so crowded.

He had to admit, he liked Sharon's apartment better than his own. There were homey touches everywhere, like a collection of mix-matched coffee mugs, prints of Impressionist paintings in the bathroom, and a homemade throw rug in the entrance. As he enjoyed the warm, inviting atmosphere of the place, he couldn't deny how unlike a home his own apartment was. Since his mom's passing and the whole debacle with Amanda, he'd thrown himself into his work, and so he had never gotten around to decorating his apartment. It was ridiculous to put time and funds into a place he barely lived in, or so he'd always thought. But now that he had Sharon's home for comparison, he realized how cold and empty his own place was. He found himself wishing that he didn't have to go back home, and that he could spend the night here.

There was a soft touch on his shoulder, and he turned to see Sharon gazing up at him. "Leticia just left," she said, her voice soft.

"What were you two talking about?" Ross asked, surprised to find his own voice just as soft. It was like they had entered into a dreamy, fragile state, something that would be broken if they raised their voices.

"She's frustrated that Melanie won't get up the guts to ask Debbie out," Sharon said. She gently took the beer from Ross's hand and set it down. "Did you like them?"

"I did." Ross smiled. He'd liked all of them. "You're still my favorite, though."

"Thank God, I was starting to worry." That now-familiar teasing light came into Sharon's eyes. "You're glad I invited you then? It wasn't awkward?"

"No." Ross reached up and cupped her cheek, his thumb swiping lightly over her cheekbone. "Not at all."

For the first time in months, perhaps years, he'd had a taste of home.

12

Sharon wasn't entirely sure what was going on with Ross, but whatever it was, it seemed to make him happy. He appeared to have had a great time, and all of her friends—people she'd known for years—loved him. "I know it was outside your comfort zone," she said, looking up at him. She tried to ignore the way her heart had been thumping painfully in her chest ever since he'd put his hand on her cheek a few seconds ago. "So I'm glad that you came and enjoyed yourself. Thank you."

Ross tilted his head and stared at her. Sharon squirmed. "What?"

"Nothing." Ross shook his head and dropped his hand from her cheek. "You just might be the most considerate person I've ever met."

Sharon could feel the heat rising to her face and knew she was blushing. "I'm just… It's human decency, that's all."

"Hmmm." Ross stepped a little closer and put his hands on her hips. Sharon could feel her heart beating even faster. "I feel like such consideration should be rewarded."

"Oh?" She slid her hands up his arms, feeling the muscles underneath. "And how would I be rewarded?"

"Well…" Ross used his grip on her hips to spin her around and then pin her back against his chest, one arm snaking around her waist to keep her still. He bent down, his breath hot against her ear. "I do believe someone expressed their enthusiasm for the idea of getting tied up…"

Sharon clenched her legs together as a wave of heat pooled between them. *Oh, yes, yes please.*

"Do you want that?" Ross asked. He slowly began to knead at her breast while using his arm to pin her against him. All she could do was tip her head back against his shoulder and let him do what he wanted to her. "Hmm? Do you want me to tie you up, make you beg for me?"

He kissed down her neck, and Sharon felt her legs turn to jelly. She leaned back, putting her weight on Ross and trusting that he'd keep her upright. How had they gone from casually existing in the same space to *this* so quickly? It felt like the room had suddenly caught fire.

"Tell me what you want," Ross whispered against her skin. "I have to hear you, sweetheart."

Sweetheart. He'd called her that the other night when he'd had her pinned against the wall. She tried to tell herself that it didn't mean anything, but she couldn't help melting a little at the endearment.

"Yes," she gasped out, a little ashamed of how needy she sounded. "Yes, please, I want you to tie me up."

"Good girl," Ross said. He stopped touching her breasts and instead slid a hand into her jeans, dragging a finger along the seam of her underwear. Sharon tried to bite back her moan. "Mmm, so wet already…"

He found her clit and she cried out. Her nails dug into his skin as he thumbed open her jeans. He soon slipped his whole hand down into her wet panties, working two fingers over her. Sharon's hips bucked and she panted heavily in Ross's ear, trying to get more friction as he rubbed his fingers in tight little circles over her clit. God's sake, she still had all of her clothes on and she was in her kitchen, and he was going to… to make her come right, right there…

"Ross, Ross please," she whispered. "The, the bedroom, Ross, please, I…" Ross slipped a finger into her, his thumb pressing against her clit, and she screamed, her hips jerking wildly. It was too much but it wasn't enough, and now he was sliding a second finger inside of her, going faster and faster and oh God, oh God, oh *God*…

Sharon's entire body shuddered and she let out a low moan, sagging against Ross as her orgasm washed through her. Well, these jeans definitely needed a wash before she wore them again.

"Now that," Ross said, kissing her temple, "was beautiful."

"I thought… you were going to…" She still didn't fully have her breath back.

"Tie you up? Oh yes. But I'm going to take my time with you, so I thought we should take the edge off first."

Sharon managed to open her eyes and look up at him. Ross's eyes were dark, and there was a sly smile on his face. "What are you waiting for, then?" She whispered, challenging him.

Ross scooped her up in his arms and she laughed in surprise, holding on for dear life as he carried her into the bedroom. "Do you have any scarves?"

"Oh Lord," Sharon laughed, pointing in the direction of her closet. "In there, but if you rip them—"

"I think the only one in danger of ripping them is you." Ross rummaged through her closet and came back a moment later with two scarves. Luckily Sharon didn't wear them much. She always seemed to forget them in her mad rush out the door for work.

Laying the scarves on the bed, Ross quickly stripped, and Sharon did the same. Now was not the time for a sensual strip tease. She wanted him and wanted him now.

"Lie down and put your hands above your head," Ross instructed, his voice calm and reassuring.

Sharon did as she was told, breathing slowly and deeply as Ross carefully tied her hands to the headboard. She'd never let anyone do this to her before, partially because she'd never really *thought* of doing this before. But she trusted Ross, even if she had no idea what he was planning.

Ross finished tying her down and rocked back on his knees, just staring at her. It was like he was drinking her in, and Sharon shivered under his dark gaze. She could almost feel it on her skin like a caress.

After a silence long enough that Sharon considered asking if something was wrong, Ross slowly leaned down and kissed her. She closed her eyes, melting into the kiss, and felt one of his hands slide up her leg. For the next few minutes he didn't do much more than kiss her while slowly moving his hands over her body. It seemed he wanted to feel every inch of her, as if he was committing her to memory. His touch was feather-light and teasing. On each pass he drew closer and closer to where she wanted him, but never quite reached her core. Eventually he pulled back, leaving her gasping for air, and began to kiss his way slowly down her body.

She was starting to be glad that he'd gotten her off in the kitchen. These slow, teasing touches were driving her crazy. She couldn't imagine how frustrated she'd be if he hadn't "taken the edge off," as he'd put it.

"Ross…"

Ross simply hummed against her skin as he kissed his way down one shoulder and then across her stomach. Then he scooted down and slowly ran his mouth up her leg, stopping just short of her sex. He sucked at the pale skin on the inside of her thigh, and Sharon's hips twitched. "Ross…"

"Patience," he whispered, and leaned up to sucked her breast into his mouth.

Sharon made a strange, strangled noise that she didn't even recognize as her own voice. She arched her body, trying to get more of that sensation. He scraped his teeth lightly against her skin and she shuddered, tugging instinctively at the restraints. One of his fingers slid between her legs and gently ran through her folds, teasing her again with light touches. He switched his mouth to the other breast and then began to touch her in earnest, his fingers working over her until she was thrusting up into them.

"Yes," she gasped, trying to encourage him. She was so close. If only he'd put his fingers inside of her again, or moved just a little faster…

And then he withdrew, running his hands soothingly along her thighs.

Sharon groaned. "I was almost…"

"I know." She could feel that dark grin against her skin. "I told you, patience."

Sharon huffed and was about to say some choice words about patience when he kissed her again. His tongue slid into her mouth, and then his fingers were teasing her again. This time one of them even slipped inside of her.

He did it again, and again, bringing her to the brink, so close to satisfaction, only to snatch it away. By the fourth time he did it she was a shaking mess, practically sobbing into his mouth. Her arms pulled against the restraints, desperate to touch him.

"Please," she whispered. "Please, Ross, please…"

He withdrew his fingers again and she moaned, but then she heard the sound of a condom package ripping open and a moment later, she felt him nudging at her entrance. She spread her legs wide, inviting him in.

When he slid into her, she could have cried with relief. Neither of them had much patience left to spare. Ross set a hard, brutal pace, one that had her arching up wildly to meet his thrusts. When it came, her orgasm felt like a freight train. She was pretty sure she'd ripped the scarves in the throes of her ecstasy. And oh God, she was absolutely ruined for anyone else.

13

In his defense, it had been so long since he'd dated that he hadn't exactly realized what was happening until it was too late to stop it.

Oh sure, he knew he was going on proper dates with Sharon now, where they wined and dined and chatted for hours before going back to his or hers for sex. He smiled as he remembered a few especially fun nights, like when he'd blindfolded her. But the dates weren't just about killing time until it was appropriately dark enough outside to have sex. He loved hearing about Sharon's work and having someone to talk to about his—someone who wasn't in the medical profession, whose interest in his stories was sympathetic rather than professional. He found himself joining Sharon's friends for more nights at her house, to the point where they were asking him out to lunch on their own, sans Sharon. He hadn't mentioned his relationship with Sharon and neither had she, so as far as he was aware only Leticia knew that they were more than friends. Yet, neither of them had actually said what they were. How did Sharon feel about this?

Actually, how did he, Ross, feel about this?

The realization hit him earlier that afternoon. It was the anniversary of his mother's death. Every year, he would find a time to stop by the grave and place flowers. He usually said a few things about how his life was going, catching her up on things. He liked to think that she could hear him but, even if she couldn't, it made him feel better to talk to her.

But this year, for the first time, he wasn't going alone.

He had asked Sharon to go with him almost without thinking about it, and when she'd said yes, he'd felt such a loose and relaxing warmth in his body that he couldn't bring himself to overthink it. They had driven out that morning and left flowers on the grave. Sharon had even brought her own small bouquet. Then he'd talked, and talked, while Sharon sat there, head on his shoulder, and let him. She'd never asked him to leave, or said that she was cold or hungry, or tried to butt in. She had simply been a comforting presence by his side and had let him mourn.

He realized now how unhealthy his relationship with Amanda had been. She had forced him to put her before everything, and had guilt-tripped him when he had tried to take care of himself. She'd thrown a fit when he had tried to see his dying mother. And after it was over, she had left him scared, scarred and emotionally distant. He had let her poison future relationships before they even started. But that was over. He couldn't let Amanda—or his grief over his mother—stop him from living his life.

"Thank you," he said, threading his fingers through Sharon's as they sat in the grass.

"I'm honored that you invited me," she replied. "And I'm honored to meet you, ma'am," she added to the grave. It was part humor and part genuine, and Ross chuckled.

"C'mon." He stood and offered Sharon his hand to help her up. "My legs are starting to get numb."

Sharon laughed. "What do you want for dinner?"

"I thought it was your turn to pick a place."

Sharon shook her head. "No. Today is your day. Chinese takeout? Italian? That new Indian place around the corner?"

"Chinese takeout." That way they could eat it at Sharon's place and catch up on their favorite mystery series.

That was when it hit him. They had a television series that they watched together. Sharon's friends were now his friends. He had taken her to see his mother's grave, on the anniversary of her death. She knew what he liked to eat.

He was in a relationship with Sharon—and fast on the heels of that revelation came another.

He was in love with her.

Ross watched Sharon arrange the flowers on the grave and then stroll ahead of him to the car, already scrolling through her phone to find the number for the Chinese place.

He was in love with her. Now he just had to find a way to tell her that.

14

Sharon tapped nervously against the kitchen island. "Ross?"

Her—whatever he was, they still hadn't talked about it—emerged from her bathroom, toweling his hair dry. Sharon swallowed. God, he was handsome. "Yeah?"

She tried to keep her voice light and steady, the way she did with potential donors. "Have you seen the paper?"

"If you can call that a paper," Ross said with a snort. He walked up and took the tabloid out of her hands. It was a local imprint, which meant that it focused on the more 'local' celebrities such as the mayor—and, apparently, on handsome surgeons.

"You're in it," Sharon started to say.

"Yeah, they put me in there now and again, usually with something about how I'm still single. I've started to become known in my field—"

"If by that you mean you're starting to give lectures on the subject of medicine then yes, you're starting to become known," Sharon teased. She was proud of how far Ross had come and how respected he was.

Ross glared at her playfully. "And apparently I'm the one that actual celebrities seek out when they're in town and have twisted their ankle. So now I'm the 'surgeon to the stars' or some nonsense. Honestly, it makes me sound like a plastic surgeon or something."

"Well, here they have photographs." Sharon flipped the tabloid open. "And you're with me."

She held her breath, waiting to see Ross's reaction to the pictures. They weren't too incriminating, thankfully. Someone must have noticed that she and Ross had a habit of going to the Italian restaurant near his apartment—the same place he'd taken her on their first date—every Friday, unless a patient kept Ross away. They must have waited for them to show up and then snapped a photo. In the photo, Ross was holding open the door for her while she stepped into the restaurant. The vain part of her was glad that she was out of the cast and ankle brace and that her limp was all but gone.

"Is… is this okay?" She asked when Ross didn't say anything. "We can take a break, if you want. You should spend more time with your friends from medical school anyway. We shouldn't give them a reason to speculate."

She didn't want the world looking at him any more than it already did. Ross had been through so much and he deserved his privacy. He had lives depending on him every day, so why did people think it was okay to invade the rare snatches of private time that he had?

As it was, Ross seemed to spend half of that time crying over patents while she held him. The other night there had been a young man, no more than twenty-five. He'd gotten trapped against his car, and by the time a friend found him and rushed him to the hospital…

Ross hadn't said a word that night. He'd been silent and withdrawn. Sharon hadn't known what to say to make it better. He hadn't even touched his dinner. And now people wanted to take pictures of him? At least actors and politicians had some idea of what they were getting into when they pursued their careers. Ross was a doctor, for Christ's sake. He didn't sign up for this. She knew he was still nervous about their relationship. This was the last thing that he needed, and if she ever met the person who took those photographs, she was going to rip them a new one.

Sharon blinked. Wow. She hadn't realized that she'd grown that protective of him.

"I don't see why we should take a break," Ross said. "Unless you want to. I know this is unexpected and probably the last thing you wanted."

"The last thing I wanted? What about you?"

"I'm okay. They didn't get anything juicy. We'll just have to eat somewhere else for a while."

Sharon nodded, knees nearly buckling in relief. He didn't want to stop spending time with her. She wasn't going to lose him. "I admit I'm surprised that you're taking it so well."

"If reporters start knocking on my door, that's when you should get concerned." Ross smiled.

Sharon tried to smile back but it felt forced. She was scared of losing him. What did that mean?

15

Ross did his best not to glance at the clock again. Normally he loved his job and had to be reminded to go home, but something had been off about Sharon that morning. He wanted to get back to her and make sure that she was okay.

"Dr. Hardwick?"

He glanced up from his paperwork. Ah, paperwork. The part of the job that everyone hated. "Yes?"

Nurse Rosa smiled apologetically. "Sorry to bother you, but there's someone here to see you. She says she's a friend?"

Could Sharon have come to the office? No, she wouldn't have, not after the tabloid that morning. It could be Leticia or Melanie or even Debbie. "Tell them to come on in."

Nurse Rosa disappeared and a moment later someone else entered—but they were far from a friend.

Ross stood up, his shoulders pulling back as if he was preparing for a fight. "Amanda."

Amanda Sorrens stood in the doorway, looking barely a day older than when he'd last seen her. She had pulled back her thick, dark hair rather than allowing it to curl around her face, but everything else looked the same, down to her favoring bright red heels. "Ross. It's been so long. How are you?"

Once, he had been captivated by her deep, rich voice, as had everyone else who met her. Now, it just grated on his nerves. It was hard to believe that he'd once been in love with her. "What do you want?"

"Goodness, aren't we defensive?" Amanda replied. She helped herself to one of his chairs and sat down. "But I suppose you have a reason to be."

"And that reason is?"

"Why, Sharon Talcott, of course."

Ross tried but couldn't stop himself from freezing momentarily before he forced himself to relax. "Who?"

A slow smile spread across Amanda's face. He hated that smile. It always came right before she told him about one of her latest schemes to get information. At first, he'd thought she was clever, but over time he'd started to find her techniques invasive and underhanded. Amanda was good with people, and that meant she was good at manipulating them into doing what she wanted. "Don't play dumb with me, Ross, it never suited you. Your new girlfriend is Sharon Talcott who, unless I'm greatly mistaken—and I never am—was also your patient. You operated on her to save her leg after she was in a car crash."

"If you say so," Ross responded. He wasn't going to give Amanda an inch.

"How did that car crash occur?" Amanda asked, curling one leg underneath her. "I hear her family has a history of alcohol abuse. Was that a factor?"

Ross realized that he was grinding his teeth together and, with great effort, unclenched them. "There was no trace of alcohol in Miss Talcott's system. Both she and her friend attested to her being distracted while using a hands-free device."

"Oh, so she is your patient. Interesting."

He could have smacked himself. He'd played right into her hands. "Yes, Miss Talcott was a patient of mine, although she hasn't officially been in my care since the first couple weeks after her operation. Her physical therapist took over from there. It's nice to know that you're showing such concern for someone else's recovery, Amanda."

Amanda gave him one long, slow blink, like a Siamese cat. "You're having an affair with a patient, Ross. I saw the photos this morning."

This was it. Ross could feel the cold fear settling in the pit of his stomach. This was what he'd feared at the beginning—that someone would find out about Sharon and use it against him. He could lose everything that he had worked for. All his mother's sacrifices would be for nothing. All his years of work, the money for school, the nights spent studying instead of going out with friends, all of it would be gone.

He took a deep breath. He was never going to let Amanda know that she had gotten to him. Never.

"You really think that you can get a story out of that from just one blurry photograph and some conjecture? That's pretty low, even for you."

Amanda shrugged one shoulder and then stood up. "I know what you're doing, Ross, and it won't work. I'm going to run this story. It will be the scandal of the year. Well-respected doctor has illicit affair with patient. What *will* the hospital board say?" She tutted.

"If you're going to run this ludicrous story no matter what, then why even come here?" To gloat?"

"Maybe I thought that my old boyfriend would like to explain his side of the story."

That was the last straw. "So, you can spin my words, like you always did when we were arguing? I think I'll pass. Get out of my office."

"Ouch," Amanda said playfully. "That one really hurt, Ross, I had no idea that you were still bitter. Tell me, does she know how to do that thing with her—"

"Out."

"Because if you'll recall, I was very good at—"

"Out," Ross repeated, crossing the room and opening the door. "Now."

With a huff, Amanda strolled out the door.

Ross made sure to slam it after her.

16

She knew right away that something was off with Ross. He had said he was working late and cancelled dinner. That alone wouldn't have been a big deal, but he'd texted her about it instead of calling, which was definitely out of the ordinary. When he stopped by her apartment later—which was rapidly becoming his apartment too, seeing as half his clothes were there along with his toothbrush and several of his dog-eared Clive Cussler novels—he didn't seem to be in the mood to talk, which was also unusual. She had assumed that it had to do with a patient, but Ross had always talked to her about patients before, and this time, he wasn't saying a word.

"Do you need something to eat?" She asked. "I have leftovers I can warm up."

Ross shrugged out of his jacket. "No, I ate at the hospital."

That was another red flag. Ross hated hospital food. "Okay. Anything you want to talk about?"

Ross braced his hands on the back of the chair and breathed deeply for a moment. When he looked up at her, she was surprised to see his eyes dark with lust. "Talk about? No. Do? Yes."

They made their way to the bedroom, kissing and discarding clothing, but she could tell that something was off. "What do you want?" She whispered into his ear as he unhooked her bra. "Tell me what you want."

"Tell me what to do," he said. "Just this once, tell me what to do."

Sharon swallowed. She could do that.

"Get on the bed," she instructed. As Ross did so she climbed after him, gently pressing his hips down. "Now stay still."

She slid her mouth over him all at once, taking him as far as she could go, and she heard Ross's strangled shout. Generally, she liked to start more slowly with blowjobs, bestowing little teasing kitten licks and sucking along the shaft, but this time it was clear to her that Ross needed to be dominated, just a little. She just hoped she was up to the challenge.

Using her elbows as leverage, Sharon kept Ross's hips pinned down. "Don't move," she reminded him, and then sucked him down again.

It was kind of nice, actually, to be in charge, although she still preferred to let Ross call the shots. She liked teasing him. It was fun to hear him moan and then watch him bite his lip to keep from making too much noise. She liked the heavy feel of him on her tongue and the bittersweet taste of him in her mouth. She reached down between her legs and started fingering herself, humming around him.

She pulled off momentarily. "You can come now," she informed him, her voice husky due to her raw throat. Then she lightly licked her lips and slid back down on him and sucked as hard as she could, her tongue running up the underside of his shaft. He came with a yell. The explosion of salt on her tongue made her come as well, dripping over her fingers as she swallowed all that she could.

When she looked up, she saw that Ross was still doing his best to keep still. Sharon gave him a wolfish grin of her own.

"Good boy," she said, grinning.

17

That round had definitely been... liberating. He liked the idea of Sharon in control every once in a while.

As Ross's heart rate slowed and he could breathe more easily, he realized that Sharon was still looking at him expectantly. The sex had done wonders to ease the tension he'd felt—that awful feeling of being out of control—but it apparently hadn't gotten rid of Sharon's concern. He couldn't find it in himself to be annoyed. He knew that he was acting out of character. She had every right to be worried, and it was sweet that she had noticed.

"I'm sorry."

"What for? I orgasmed quite nicely myself, in case you didn't notice."

Ross laughed, rolling over so that he could see the mirth shining in Sharon's eyes. "No, I meant... about earlier, I was upset and wasn't talking about it."

"Do you want to talk about it now?"

"Might as well get it over with."

A part of him wanted to tell her about Amanda, but a bigger part of him didn't want to scare her. What could Sharon possibly do about it anyway except worry?

"I think we should be just a little more careful from now on about being seen together." Ross spoke slowly, hoping that he didn't sound angry or upset.

"I thought you said that it was fine?"

"It is, or it would be, but I remembered that you were originally my patient."

Sharon snorted, a habit she'd picked up from him no doubt. "That hardly counts, we met before I was your patient. It was just an unfortunate series of coincidences."

Ross raised his hand to casually play with Sharon's hair. She relaxed further into his chest, tucking her head underneath his chin. "Maybe, but the truth is that I wouldn't have tracked you down if you hadn't been my patient. It's a bit of a gray area. I think, just to be safe, we should lay low for a while."

"Lay low?" Sharon chuckled. "You make it sound like we're bandits or something."

Ross laughed as well, but it sounded hollow to him. "Just for my peace of mind, okay? I know I'm being paranoid…"

"This is your medical license we're talking about," Sharon interrupted. "It's perfectly okay, Ross. You worked your whole life to earn this position, I'm not letting anyone take it away from you."

The ferocity in her voice surprised him. "I hope you know how much I appreciate your consideration. It's…" He struggled to find the words. "Refreshing. New."

"I care about you," Sharon replied. "It's the least I can do."

And I love you for thinking it's the least you can do, Ross thought. Amanda would never have thought of hiding their relationship as a small thing. She never would have considered his happiness, or how this might affect his job. But Sharon did.

He really should get around to telling her that he loved her. But while the thought floated through his mind on a daily basis, the idea of actually saying it out loud made him feel a bit faint. He'd said those words to Amanda all the time—too many times. He had said them as if they were an obligation, not because he genuinely felt them. On the other hand, he hadn't said those words enough to Mom. He should have made sure she knew before she passed that he could never replace the guidance, unconditional love, and support she had given him.

He wanted to tell Sharon that he loved her, if only for the sake of his mother's memory. He knew what it was like to lose someone that he loved and feel the weight of so many missed opportunities. Sharon had already been in one car crash, and that reminded him that he might, through illness or accident, lose her someday. But Amanda's ghost haunted him just as strongly as his mother's, especially now that she had popped back into his life.

Ross kept himself still so that he didn't disturb Sharon, but inside he was tossing and turning. What was he supposed to do?

18

Sharon pursed her lips as she read through the barrage of emails that inevitably awaited her at the start of each work day. Time to metaphorically roll up her sleeves and reassure everybody that contrary to their fears, the charity was running fine and nothing was on fire.

"Excuse me," She heard Charlene say outside her door, "Sorry, you can't go in—"

The door to Sharon's office burst open and a tall woman with thick, dark hair and an oily smile stood there. Behind the woman, Charlene was glaring.

"So sorry to bother you," the woman said in a tone that indicated she wasn't sorry at all. "Do you mind if I take a moment of your time?"

"Are you selling Bibles?" Sharon asked. The woman had a very *have you heard of our Lord and Savior* tone.

The woman arched one eyebrow in a way that she probably thought was elegant. "My, my, I see he still likes the feisty ones."

Something about that set off alarm bells in Sharon's head. She looked over at Charlene. "It's okay, I'm fine."

Charlene nodded, then sent a final glare at the woman's back before retreating and shutting the door behind her. The woman crossed the room to Sharon, her hand out to shake. "I'm Amanda. It's lovely to meet you. Ross told me a lot about you."

Sharon shook Amanda's hand but stayed behind her desk. "You must be his ex. The journalist. What do you want?"

"Cutting to the chase, I like it." Amanda sat on Sharon's desk, thankfully not on top of any paperwork. "I'm here to have a little chat, girl to girl."

"Will this little chat end up in newsprint?" Sharon replied. Normally when it came to break ups, Sharon liked to get both sides of the story. Oftentimes it was the fault of both parties, even though each tried to demonize the other afterwards to soothe their own wounded pride and broken heart. But she trusted Ross's judgment, and even if she didn't, she could smell a rat a mile away.

Amanda heaved a sigh, as if she were giving away a huge secret. "To tell you the truth, Sharon—do you mind if I call you Sharon?—you're going to end up in newsprint whether you talk to me or not. Somebody found out that you were Ross's patient and they're going to expose him. I'm trying to do you a favor and get in ahead, so people know your side of the story."

Sharon's first reaction was to freeze as icy dread began to fill her limbs. No. Everything Ross had worked for, his entire life, was about to become fodder for gossip. Her second reaction was rage. She knew, without a doubt, that Amanda was the one behind this exposé.

She liked to think of herself as a calm and rational person. She wouldn't be in public relations if she wasn't able to keep her temper. It was her job to face the public, and that meant donors and reporters alike, no matter how daunting it might be. But every once in a while, her Irish roots came out and she found herself full of a burning fury that seemed to fill every inch of her. It made her hands shake.

Her hands were definitely shaking now.

"And who would be motivated to turn this into a story?" Sharon replied. She folded her arms to hide the trembling of her hands. She wanted to strangle this woman. "I don't suppose Ross's bitter ex would have any reason to drag his name through the mud, would she?"

Amanda's lips started to curl back into a snarl, but then Sharon could see her visibly compose herself. "I go where the story is."

"And there's barely any story here. You're not a very good actress, you know. Why do you hate Ross so much that you'd try to get him fired?"

"This has nothing to do with any feelings I may or may not have towards Ross. This isn't personal. This is business. And it makes for a great story." Amanda clucked her tongue. "Poor Ross. I went to warn him, you know, for old time's sake. He just kicked me out."

"Well allow me to follow his example. They say couples start to pick up each other's habits, you know." Sharon rose and swiftly crossed the room, wrenching the door open in her haste to be rid of

Amanda. "Get out of my office, and don't even think of setting foot in here again."

Amanda stood fluidly, like a cat, and exited. "I just hope you're worth it to him," she called over her shoulder, "Seeing as you might cost him his job."

It took every ounce of self-control that Sharon had not to slam the door in the woman's face—or, even better, to chase after her and give her a black eye.

"Everything okay?" Charlene asked, looking up from her desk.

Sharon closed her eyes and took a deep breath. "Everything's fine."

Or, at least she hoped that it would be.

19

For the second time in as many days, Ross was interrupted in the middle of paperwork. This time, his intruder was much more welcome.

"Miss Talcott!" he said, standing quickly and ushering her in so that he could close the door. "What are you doing here?" He asked in a much quieter voice once the door was shut. "I thought that we agreed to keep this on the down low for now."

"I got a visit today from Amanda," Sharon replied.

Ross clenched his jaw. That *bitch*. "What did she say?"

"A lot of things. Most of them I ignored, and then I showed her the door. But she told me something very interesting." Sharon's eyes were blazing, and although she kept her voice low, Ross could tell that she was angry—really, truly angry. It reminded him of her reaction when he'd stopped by Dr. Chavez's place to see her, only much worse. "She said that she was writing an exposé about us. As if that wasn't horrifying enough, she also told me she'd already talked to you about it." Sharon folded her arms. "I'd like to believe that she told you this morning, but since she stopped by right as I was starting my work day, I'd say that's pretty impossible."

Ross took a deep breath. Hoo boy.

"You knew that she was going to drag your name through the mud and you didn't tell me?" There was something vulnerable about Sharon's gaze, despite her anger. "I'm supposed to be your partner, Ross. You need to tell me things like this."

"I wanted to protect you. There wasn't anything that you could do to stop this from happening, and I didn't want you to worry."

"So that I could be blindsided by it when the story was printed in the paper?" Sharon was clearly struggling to keep her voice down so the words came out with a hiss. "Ross, there's a difference between protecting someone and being unfair or dishonest, and this was both! You withheld information from me—information that directly affects me! You did nothing to prepare me for when this story drops!"

Ross couldn't help his instinctive desire to defend himself. It rose up inside his throat like bile. This reminded him of Amanda's frequent tantrums, when she would shout and throw things and make him terrified that the neighbors would hear. He had to close his throat a little and breathe through his nose. This wasn't Amanda. This was Sharon, who had shown him nothing but consideration and thoughtfulness. Sharon, who had respected his boundaries and given him her trust and faith. Sharon who introduced him to her friends, and worked around his crazy schedule, and let him into her home without question.

"I'm sorry." He took another deep breath. "It feels like I'm saying that a lot lately. And I'm going to be saying it a lot more often once this story hits."

"No, no, no." Sharon came forward and took his face gently in her hands. "This is just as much my fault as it is anyone's. I should have said no to the first date. I should have waited until my leg was fully healed."

"We've been dating for months," Ross growled. "How can anyone think that it's just a fling or an affair, how can anyone… If it was Dr. Chavez you'd been sleeping with, maybe, but…"

Sharon laughed, her thumbs gently stroking his skin. "And I'm sure everyone with half a brain will realize that. Including your superiors."

"I don't know." Ross didn't want to dash her hopes, but he owed it to her to be honest. "They'll be more worried about the story itself, I think, than what's actually true. If enough people believe the story and start pressuring the hospital to do something, I could get the boot just to shut them up and preserve the hospital's funding."

Sharon sucked in a harsh breath. "Just for that? Cowards."

Ross gazed down into her fierce, open face. "God, I love you."

Sharon stared up at him, and he slowly came to the realization that he'd said that out loud. "What?"

"I…"

Sharon's thumbs stopped moving and she drew one hand away, using it to cover her eyes. "Sorry, I'm sorry, I just—I didn't expect you—"

"To feel it or to say it?"

"Both? I don't know." Sharon dropped her hand and he could see that her eyes were moist. "This has been quite a day, huh?"

"And it's not even lunch yet."

Sharon laughed thickly, then pulled him closer for a light kiss. "C'mon, I'm going to get you some proper non-hospital food."

"But the paperwork…"

"Can wait." She winked at him and started to lead him out the door. Ross knew, without a doubt, that he'd follow wherever she led him.

And that he wanted to follow where she led for the rest of his life.

20

Once again, Sharon mused, she was calling Leticia in a panic about Ross. But at least this time she was freaking out about a man she'd been dating for a good few months, rather than a one-night stand.

"Everything okay?" Leticia asked when she picked up the phone. "You don't usually call while I'm still at work."

Sharon glanced at the clock on the mantle and realized that it was 6:00 PM on a Friday, which meant that Leticia was taking care of paperwork for an extra couple of hours after the museum was closed before heading out to the clubs. "Sorry, I didn't realize the time."

"Uh-huh. And don't think I can't hear the dead tone in your voice. Something's up."

Sharon sighed. "You're going to want to sit down."

"I already am."

She quickly explained everything that had happened. To her credit, Leticia didn't interrupt once. Sharon always forgot that, while Leticia was loud most of the time, she became quiet and laser-focused when it came to the important things.

"So, what's the problem?" Leticia finally asked after Sharon had fallen silent.

"You mean other than the fact that my relationship is about to be exposed to the entire city and that Ross might lose his job?"

"Oh c'mon," Leticia groaned. "You and I both know that's not the real issue. I'm with you—this thing will blow over. And if the hospital board doesn't have the sense to see that Amanda is sensationalizing this, they don't deserve Ross anyway. I mean, he could make a fortune as a consultant, first of all. Second of all, there are other hospitals in Pittsburgh, and outside of it. He can go somewhere else. It's not fun, but it's not the end of the world. No, something else is eating you. Cough it up."

Sharon thought for a moment, trying to get her thoughts into order. "It feels like things are going too fast."

"In what way?"

"Just that… we haven't even really talked about what we are. We've been dating for months but—I mean, he told me that he loved me for the first time today."

"Do you love him back?"

Sharon paused. Was she in love with Ross?

She recalled the way in which he always seemed to know what she wanted in the bedroom, and the fact that she trusted him there in a way she hadn't been able to trust anyone else. She thought of her fierce desire to protect him, and how she wanted to strangle Amanda for hurting him. She remembered the hours spent in restaurants, the extra toothbrush in her apartment, and the ease with which he fit into her group of friends. She thought of his predatory grin, his soft eyes, and how safe she felt sleeping in his arms.

"Yes, I am, it's just… I'm worried that I'm falling too quickly and this is all happening too fast—"

"Stop worrying," Leticia advised. "You two have done well so far. And let's be honest here, the others all know you're dating. I know you two try to hide it around them, but the way that you two look at each other is sickening. In the best way, of course."

There was a knock at the door and Sharon got up to answer it. "Are you sure? I'm not losing my mind?"

"I think that you two have been in love for a while. He's just been too scared and you've been too respectful of his boundaries to acknowledge it."

Sharon opened the door to find Ross standing there. "Ross?"

"Yes?" Ross looked confused. "It's Friday."

Friday. Their date night. They had a longstanding date night.

"Leticia? I have to go." Sharon hung up before she could hear her friend's undoubtedly indignant reply.

Maybe they weren't moving too fast or falling too hard. Maybe they'd already fallen in love—and into each other's lives—a long time ago, without even realizing it.

21

Ross could feel the weight of the small box in his pocket. It was strange, how everything had fallen into place once he'd thought about it. He had realized that he wanted to follow Sharon everywhere, and that he never wanted to be apart from her. And they'd been together, even if they'd never strictly admitted it, for a number of months now.

He had never felt as safe or as considered as he did with Sharon. He felt like he had a say in the relationship rather than desperately trying to deal with a whirlwind. And now, with the tabloid story hanging over their heads, what better way to circumvent the gossip and establish that Sharon was truly, permanently in his life than to propose?

All right, so maybe it was a little sudden, and maybe he was rushing it. But it didn't feel like a rush—not when he'd been in denial about the serious nature of their relationship for a long while. He was practically living with her, for crying out loud. He was in love with Sharon. And he wanted to make it official.

Since they were trying to lay low, he didn't want to do anything fancy. Certainly nothing public. So he got his mother's ring reset and spent the next week planning what he was going to say.

He took Sharon out the following Friday. Neither of them had heard from Amanda since last week, but they both knew that the story was coming at some point. It was just a matter of when.

Ross tried not to think about that. Instead, he focused on how beautiful Sharon looked that night, wearing the same dress she'd worn on the night they'd met. It was apt, he thought, if coincidental, that she'd chosen to wear it.

They hadn't gone to their usual Italian place, unfortunately, since Amanda or someone else might be lying in wait there. Instead they'd driven separately across town to a little Mexican place that they'd heard about from Debbie. "Hey," he suggested once they got their bill, "Why don't we go for a walk? I hear there's a lovely park just down the street."

Sharon looked up at him. "Are you sure that's wise?"

"Nobody knows us around here," Ross reassured her. "I think it'll be nice."

Sharon still looked a little nervous, but she nodded.

The park was lovely, which Ross knew because he'd scoped it out earlier that week. It had been Tom who told him about it. Ross had wanted to know if there were any scenic green spaces in the area that wouldn't be too crowded, and Tom had naturally known the answer.

Ross led the way down a side path that, conveniently, took them right past the art gallery where they'd first met. "Hey, I think it's open." he said, grinning as he pointed to the gallery. "Want to stop inside?"

"Sure, why not," Sharon said, matching his smile with one of her own. "Maybe they'll have art I actually like this time."

That sparked a playful argument about art as they made their way into the gallery (Tom and Leticia had pulled some strings to make sure the gallery would be open just for them) and through the first couple of rooms.

"Sharon…" Ross could feel his heart hammering in his chest. He hadn't been this nervous since his first medical exam. "This is where we met. This is where a new chapter of my life began, even if it took me a long time to realize it."

Sharon paused, seeming to realize that something serious was happening. Ross did his best to keep his voice steady as he continued.

"I've kind of dragged my feet on this, haven't I? It took me forever to tell you I love you, or even to admit that we were dating. I only realized last week that I've moved in with you."

Sharon laughed at that. "I knew you'd catch on eventually, but I didn't want to say anything in case I was wrong."

"See, that's exactly it." Ross found himself starting to relax. As always, Sharon understood. "I've had so many walls up, and you've been so good about respecting them. You never took any bullshit from me, but you gave me the space I needed, and I appreciate that. Now I've realized that you're in my life and in my heart, completely."

He knelt down, carefully pulling the small box out of his pocket. He'd wanted to use his mother's ring, but he had gotten it reset so that it would be unique to Sharon. The past and the future merging together. "I want to make us official and permanent, because I honestly don't know what I'd do without you."

Sharon gasped, her hand flying up to her mouth. "But… but the papers. The board. Ross, there's no hiding this. You could lose your practice."

"I know. I like to think that my marrying you will help them see that this isn't just an affair, but I don't know and I don't think I care. You're more important to me."

"But…" Sharon looked like she might cry. "You've worked your whole life for this."

"My work isn't who I am. I can find another hospital. I can consult, or I can teach. But I can't replace you. So…" Ross cleared his throat. "Will you marry me?"

Now Sharon really was starting to cry. "Yes, okay—I mean, if you're sure, then yes, yes, yes."

Ross jumped to his feet and reeled her to him. He kissed her deeply—not the easiest task, given that they were both laughing and, in Sharon's case, still crying a bit.

He slipped the ring onto her finger.

Perfect.

22

Sharon hadn't been sure what to expect when she'd gathered everyone at her apartment to break the news of her engagement. Even though Leticia had told her that they all knew she was dating Ross, and that she wasn't fooling anyone, she had worried that they'd feel betrayed.

Apparently, she needn't have worried.

"Happy six-month anniversary!" Tom said as he entered, carrying potato chips.

"What he said," Melanie added, coming in behind him.

"I take it Leticia told you we're no longer in denial," Sharon replied.

"Oh, don't look so upset, we all knew anyway." Melanie gave her a sloppy kiss on the cheek. "Now we can just show you that we know!"

"Well, there's something you all don't know," Sharon said, leading the twins into the living room where the others were already gathered.

"What, did he pop the question or something?" Debbie said, snorting into her drink.

When Sharon was silent, everyone stared—except for Leticia and Tom, who exchanged glances that looked suspiciously knowing. Jonas almost dropped his beer.

"Did he?" Leticia demanded.

Sharon took the ring out of her pocket and slipped it on to her hand.

Her friends, predictably, exploded.

Laughing, Sharon gave them a recap of Ross's proposal. "I'm worried it's rather sudden," she admitted.

"It wouldn't be so sudden if you two had admitted you were in love in the first place," Leticia shot back.

"You don't seem all that surprised," Sharon pointed out to her, gesturing at Tom as well.

"How do you think that gallery happened to be open so long after its closing hours, not to mention conveniently empty?" Tom replied, winking at her.

"You're lucky I was in on it," Leticia cut in, "Tom here wanted to hide in the corner and take photos. I informed him that you'd strangle him with his own tie."

Sharon opened her mouth to reply, but then she felt her phone vibrating in her pocket. "Excuse me."

She left her friends to their gushing and went into the bedroom. It was Ross. "Hey, everything okay?"

"I'm being called before the board." There was more exhaustion in his voice than she'd ever heard there before. "Amanda was kind enough to send them a copy."

"That bitch," Sharon yelled before she could stop herself. "Sorry," she added more quietly. "They're calling you up?"

"Yeah." Ross sighed again. "Tomorrow morning. Emergency hearing. So, I don't think I'll get to see you beforehand."

"When will you finish?"

"I think around noon?"

"Then I'll be there when you get out." Sharon clenched her hands into fists to keep them from shaking. "We'll get through this."

They would get through this. They would. Even if she had to knock some sense into the board herself.

"What's going on?" Melanie asked, knocking softly on the door. "Sharon? Everything okay?"

Sharon opened the door to see Melanie peering at her in what Sharon called her friend's 'therapy face.'

"Ross is getting called before the board because of our relationship," she said quietly. "I was technically his patient and so this—this journalist, his ex-girlfriend, has turned it into some sordid doctor-patient affair thing."

"What?" Melanie's features hardened. "I should have expected this. Abusive partners try to find a way to get back into your life and exert control over you again. That's what they want, control. Even if, rationally, they know that they'll never have that power over you again, they can't help themselves—if they can't control you, they'll make sure they have your attention at the very least."

Sharon sighed. "You can't predict what every asshole person is going to do, Mel, that's not how being a therapist works."

The hard set of Melanie's mouth said, clear as day, that she *should* be able to predict what every asshole person was going to do, and that this was somehow her fault for not knowing.

Sharon pushed past her—not angrily, just restless and not sure what to do. This had to be fixed, somehow. She couldn't be the reason that Ross lost everything. And maybe Leticia had been right that there were other hospitals, other cities, and other opportunities, but Ross didn't deserve to have his life uprooted just because he'd had sex with the wrong girl at the wrong time.

And it was all her fault, wasn't it? If she hadn't been distracted and taken that turn too fast, she wouldn't have crashed, and none of this would be an issue.

But you wouldn't be with Ross, said the little voice in the back of her head that sounded annoyingly like Leticia. Sharon and Ross had gotten together again because of her surgery. He wouldn't be in her life right now if that hadn't happened.

Sharon didn't know what to think or do. She felt torn between her irritation at herself, her fear for Ross, and a guilty sense of gratitude that she still got to be with him, despite the repercussions. Either her thoughts shown plainly on her face as she stepped into the living room, or it was Melanie hovering behind her like a concerned ghost that gave her away. The others could clearly tell that something was amiss.

"Hey, babe, what's wrong?" Jonas asked, hurrying over and guiding her towards the couch.

"Ross's hearing," Sharon told them, because they were her friends and she trusted them. Besides, they were going to ferret it out of her anyway, especially once they got some drinks in her—and they would, because she was feeling miserable and, like a responsible adult, planned to drown her worries in a fuckton of wine. "It's tomorrow. Amanda, his ex, she's a journalist and she sent them a copy of the exposé—the board, I mean—and they're having an emergency hearing tomorrow."

"Tomorrow?" Debbie immediately perked up. "That's sudden. Ross doesn't get any time to prepare a defense."

"They'll kick him out," Jonas said, always the gloomy one. "If they're not giving him any time to prepare, it's because they've already made up their minds and they just want it over and done with. Institutions will do anything to avoid a scandal."

That had been her concern as well—that the board was calling this meeting so quickly because they just wanted to get rid of Ross and sweep this whole thing under the rug. Hadn't Ross predicted something like this would happen? And had it really only been a few weeks ago that Amanda had walked back into Ross's life? It felt like so much longer and so much shorter all at the same time. But then, Sharon felt like she could measure her time with Ross both in years and in a handful of days, and her first meeting with him seemed to have taken place a lifetime ago, or perhaps only yesterday. She supposed that was what it felt like when you were in love.

"Thank you, Jonas," Leticia said, putting an arm around Sharon's shoulders, "For your thoughtful comment. That was super helpful. Totally lifted our spirits."

Jonas, by way of apology, passed Sharon a glass of wine.

"What exactly did Amanda write in this exposé that would make them consider firing Ross?" Debbie asked.

Sharon sighed, indulging herself by taking a gulp of wine. Melanie and Tom sat down together in the chair off to one side, watching her with identically solemn expressions. "Ross and I slept together the night that I had my accident—literally just before it happened. I was on my way home from his place when I crashed the car. Ross operated on me, but he didn't recognize me at the time, so he didn't know that I was a potential conflict of interest until afterwards. Then we started dating even though we shouldn't have because I was still kind of his patient—"

"But did he see you regularly as your doctor?" Debbie asked.

"No, just once for a follow-up checkup. I've been working with the physical therapist, mostly."

Debbie was opening her phone and scrolling through something. "When's his hearing tomorrow?"

"I don't know," Sharon said. "I'd have to check—Deb, what are you doing?"

Melanie got a knowing smile on her face, her gaze flicking over to Debbie. "Sharon, darling, I think you've forgotten Deb's profession."

"Get me the time of the hearing," Debbie said, tapping rapidly on her phone. "Technically I don't think he needs a lawyer present, but they're already setting a precedent by giving him such short notice, and it can only help."

"Are you serious?" Sharon couldn't believe her ears. And maybe that was just an expression, but she genuinely wondered if maybe she had misheard Debbie, or if she'd had more alcohol than she'd thought and was actually smashed right now, or if she was even asleep and having a stress dream about this. "Debbie, I can't ask you to do this."

"You're not asking me, I'm offering." Debbie continued to tap away on her phone. "And I don't mind. You and Ross are engaged, for fuck's sake. That's a hell of a lot more than an affair. The prosecution's argument is shaky at best."

"There's our little shark," Melanie said fondly.

"Don't you have work tomorrow?" Sharon pointed out.

"Not anymore, I don't," Debbie replied. She put her phone up to her ear. "Hello, Cynthia?" Debbie coughed, her voice sounding frail and wrecked. "Yeah, I'm so sorry, but I don't think I should come into work tomorrow. One of those twenty-four-hour flu things, I think." She coughed again, a great big one that made her chest shake. "Ugh, God, yeah, I just feel awful. No, of course, I'll get plenty of sleep. Thank you so much, Cynthia. Haha, yeah, probably overwork from the Ladimeer case. I feel you." Another cough. "Okay, thanks, goodnight!"

Debbie hung up and looked over at Sharon. "There, now I'm free tomorrow. Anyone else busy?"

"I don't have clients until the afternoon," Melanie said.

"I make my own hours," Tom pointed out.

"I'm used to a lack of sleep," Leticia said, which, considering her clubbing habits, was more than fair.

"Fuck it," Jonas said eloquently.

"All right." Debbie clapped her hands together. "Does Ross have a copy of this article that Amanda wrote? Because I need that."

"I can get it if Ross doesn't have it," Leticia said. "I know someone in Amanda's office. They've worked with me on articles about the museum."

"Melanie, you're a therapist, I need you to get all records of Sharon's medical files. You know, as her doctor, helping her through the psychological trauma of this accident."

"This is borderline illegal, you guys all know that, right?" Sharon pointed out.

"We wouldn't have to do borderline illegal things to get this information if they'd given us more time," Debbie said cheerfully, "But since they're assholes, we do what we have to."

"For a lawyer, you're very willing to bend the law."

"The best way to know how to break the rules is to learn what the rules are, and then you can break them strategically," Debbie replied.

"We should make sure someone writes an article in rebuttal," Jonas pointed out, getting his phone out of his pocket and starting to type rapidly. "Ross is being treated unfairly. If the rest of the world sees Amanda for what she really is, then she'll stop, right? Isn't that what you always say, Mel, that abusers stop when their actions are subject to public observation because they know what they're doing is wrong?"

"That's the gist of it, yes," Melanie said.

"There should be music swelling right now," Leticia declared. "Big, inspirational, go get 'em music."

"This isn't a movie," Sharon muttered, blushing. "Although you all seem determined to make it one."

"Well where do you think movies get their inspiration?" Debbie replied. "Now, I want you to grab a notebook or a computer or something and write down everything that happened, in order, for the court. I'll be editing it, by the way, gotta make sure that the phrasing is exactly right—"

Sharon's head was spinning a little, and she knew it had nothing to do with the wine. She'd only taken one sip, after all. "Uh, okay, can we slow down?"

Leticia, bless her, took the wine glass from Sharon's hand and then took Sharon's hands in hers as she sat down next to her on the couch. "Honey, I know that this is making you feel a little like you want to vomit."

Sharon nodded.

"And it's all moving really quickly, and you've got all of these changes and new information flying at you," Leticia went on.

Sharon nodded, feeling tears prick at her eyes. She felt like such a child, but Leticia was her best friend for a reason—more like family in some ways—and she knew Sharon better than anyone. Perhaps even better than Sharon's own parents knew her.

Leticia sighed and pulled Sharon into a hug, while the other four quietly worked on their phones and jotted down notes. Melanie was on the phone with someone, speaking in a low voice as she moved into the kitchen.

"You two finally admit that you're in love with each other, and the next thing you know, you're engaged. Of course it feels fast," Leticia explained, smoothing her hand through Sharon's hair. "And now this stupid hearing is coming right on top of it, and it's all just overwhelming, isn't it?"

Sharon nodded.

"How about you just write down everything that happened," Leticia said. "I'll help, since you were telling me about it the whole time, and then we can bundle you off to bed."

Part of her really liked that idea. She was tired. She had gone from the adrenaline rush of telling everyone about her engagement to the sick, swooping roller coaster feeling of learning about Ross's hearing, to the strange, swelling feeling in her chest as she watched her friends literally call off their jobs so they could help her. It was a lot to process.

But she didn't want to just go to sleep, not when they had only so much time before Ross's hearing. She couldn't just leave her friends to do all of the work for her. Ultimately, this concerned Ross and her, not them, and if they were going to stay up to get Ross through this, then she would as well.

She sat up, taking Leticia's hand and squeezing it gratefully. "No, no I need to help too. I'll write down the sequence of events, Deb, no problem."

"Be sure to emphasize that there was a romantic connection," Debbie said, not looking up from her phone, "And if there was any hanky-panky while you were in the hospital, feel free to leave that out."

Sharon could feel her face heating up. Debbie noticed her blush out of the corner of her eye and looked up, scandalized. "Jesus, I was joking. Did you seriously get it on in the hospital?"

Sharon cleared her throat. "It's not like I don't know about you getting it on with the Klingon girl at Comic Con that one year."

"Jesus Christ," Debbie muttered, looking back at her phone. "Just make this report as sanitized and lovey-dovey as possible, okay? And mention the proposal: exactly what he said, how he planned it, all of that. We need to show the board that you two are in a serious and committed relationship. Also, you two have moved in together, right?"

"My name is the only one on the apartment, but yes."

"Oh, we gotta change that. What time is it? Is your landlord awake?"

Sharon blanched. "Deb, you can't go bother my landlord!"

"I think she already is," Jonas noted as Debbie made her way to the door and slipped her shoes on.

"I'll go with her," Melanie said hurriedly, hanging up her phone. Debbie was already out the door, and Melanie had to jog to catch up with her. "Deb, babe, we agreed…"

Babe? Sharon mouthed at Tom, who shrugged. If Melanie and Debbie had finally stopped dancing around each other, it seemed that Tom hadn't heard about it. Sharon looked over at Leticia. "She can't possibly get the landlord to put Ross's name on the apartment, can she?"

"If anyone can, it's Debbie." Leticia smiled comfortingly. "If anyone can do any of this, it's Debbie. You're our friend, Sharon. Let us help you out, okay? Lord knows you've always been there for us."

Sharon nodded. Maybe, just maybe, they could all band together and actually pull this off.

23

Ross didn't want to go back to his own place that night. He knew it was the smart thing to do, but he just couldn't face the large, empty apartment. Sharon would probably already be asleep, and he'd have to get up and leave before she woke up in the morning, but he just wanted to be able to hold her. As he climbed the stairs to her—their—apartment, he imagined how that Sharon would look spread out on the bed. He didn't know if it was a holdover from the weeks she spent wearing a cast, but Sharon tended to sleep on her back with her injured leg straightened out and to the side, which meant that Ross couldn't really spoon her. But at least he could sleep tucked into her side, with his arm over her waist. He already looked forward to the idea of burying his nose in her hair to smell her shampoo, and to seeing the engagement ring glint on her finger.

But when he got to the apartment door, he saw that there was light seeping out underneath it. Had Sharon left the light on for him? Had she perhaps fallen asleep on the couch, waiting for him to come back? He'd said that he probably wouldn't see her before the hearing, but maybe Sharon had waited up for him anyway, just in case. Or perhaps she hadn't understood that he meant he was going to go back to his apartment. Honestly, considering that he was standing here in front of Sharon's apartment after all, maybe Sharon knew him better than he knew himself.

He opened the door, prepared to carry a sleepy Sharon off to bed—and goodness knew how much sleeping on the couch would make her leg ache in the morning—only to be greeted by the sight of six slightly guilty-looking people all crowded on the couch.

Ross stood there in the doorway, feeling slightly stupid, and took in the scene. Debbie was apparently holding court in the middle of the couch, papers spread out around her. Some of the papers looked like contracts or other legal documents, a few looked like they were articles out of a magazine or newspaper, and still others were handwritten notes. Sitting on Debbie's left was Jonas, tapping wildly on his phone in accordance with orders that Debbie was issuing to him. Melanie was standing behind Debbie, pointing at various papers and dictating to Tom, who was sitting alone on the chair and typing on a computer. Sharon was sitting on Debbie's right, trying to organize the papers into a stack, and Leticia was sitting on the arm of the couch, talking to somebody on the phone.

"Okay, my friend said that she can put the For Sale up on the website but that the timestamp will still show that it's from tonight and so it'll look last-minute," Leticia said.

"Doesn't matter. This isn't a real court case, so nobody's going to look that closely at the timestamp," Debbie replied. "As long as his apartment is listed as being for sale, that's all that matters."

"'She also displays the classic obsessive behavior of an abuser, seeking to exert control over her current and former victims in order to feel…'" Melanie went on.

"Hold on, I can only type so fast, I'm an artist, woman, not a secretary," Tom grouched.

"Where the hell is the stapler, we need to get these into some kind of order," Sharon said, exasperated, wrestling with a pile of paper. "Honestly, we're going to have to type all of these up. Deb, is this how you organize your cases? No wonder you never sleep."

That was when everyone saw him, and all turned to look. Leticia started smirking, Tom was still typing and didn't even realize what was happening, Melanie stopped mid-sentence, and both Jonas and Debbie's mouths fell open.

Sharon turned, saw him, and jumped to her feet. "Oh my God, I thought—you said—you're supposed to be at your apartment."

"That's up for sale, by the way," Leticia piped up. "You don't mind that you now co-own this apartment with Sharon, do you?"

"I… what?" Ross said faintly. "What is this?"

"I'm sorry," Sharon blurted, hurrying over. "They're very determined."

"This is true, we are," Jonas said, apparently not feeling sorry in the slightest.

"Finished," Tom said, finally looking up. "Hey, Ross."

"Hey Tom." Ross said, trying not to laugh. He looked back at Sharon. "Seriously, what's going on? Not that I mind the, uh, co-owning bit, we were going to officially complete this move anyway, but why…?"

"It's because of your hearing tomorrow," Sharon said, sighing. "Debbie's a lawyer and she's decided to represent you."

"I don't know if that's necessary," Ross pointed out. "It's just me and the board…"

"But if you walk in with an attorney to advise you, they'll know that you're serious. They want to sweep you under the rug so that they don't have to worry about a backlash, instead of actually doing this properly." Debbie went back to looking at her notes. "If you come in with me and let me speak for you, or at least with you, they'll see that you're prepared to fight, and they'll be more willing to listen what you have to say."

Ross felt a little overwhelmed, and Sharon gave a little laugh. "I know, I know, you have the same look on your face that I must have earlier."

She wrapped her arms around his neck and Ross put an arm around her waist instinctively, ready to hold her up. She'd been sitting for a while, so her leg might not be bothering her, but he wanted to hold her just in case it gave out.

"Awww," Leticia said, finally hanging up the phone. "Somebody take a photo of this."

Ross tightened his arm around Sharon's waist as she glared at Leticia. "It really would be better if you had Debbie there with you," Sharon said quietly, just for him. "She'll be able to present this better than we can. This is what she's used to."

"You really don't have to do this," Ross said, looking at all of them. "Honestly, all of you, this isn't your issue."

"It's Sharon's issue," Jonas said, "And that means that it's our issue. And Sharon loves you."

"Oh, yeah, welcome to the family, by the way," Tom said casually. Ross wanted to laugh at how nonchalant Tom seemed about all of this. "We usually hold a big party but we figure saving your ass is a suitable replacement."

"You're all assholes," Sharon mumbled, turning to bury her face in Ross's chest. "They're all assholes and I don't know why I put up with any of them."

"I don't know, I think they're pretty okay," Ross replied. Then he scooped her up, making Sharon squeak in surprise and cling to him, which made all the others in the room laugh and make kissy noises.

Ross ignored them, walking over to the couch and sinking onto it with Sharon on his lap. "I hate you, too," Sharon added rather unconvincingly.

"I know," Ross said cheerfully. "So," he said, looking at the others, "What have we got?"

None of them except Sharon and Jonas got any sleep. Sharon tried valiantly to stay awake, but she eventually dropped off in Ross's lap as Debbie explained her plans for the hearing. Ross carried her into bed while Jonas said his goodbyes to everyone in the living room. He was the only one of them used to a decent sleep schedule and with office hours that he couldn't change.

Sharon clung to him in her sleep as he tried to lay her down on the bed. Their bed, he thought. The one that Sharon had bought in a king size because she could, and because sometimes Leticia would crash there and sleep over. The one with light blue sheets and tons of ridiculously comfortable pillows.

Ross tucked her in, making sure that her leg was stuck out the right way and that she was on her back so she wouldn't roll over it in her sleep. She looked beautiful like this. She looked beautiful all the time, actually, but this was something different. Sharon almost always had worry lines around her forehead, or her mouth, or in the corners of her eyes, but now they were all smoothed by sleep. He wished that she could look like this all the time.

She didn't deserve to be dragged into this. He shouldn't have kept seeing her. There was no way that Amanda or anyone else would have known about their one-night stand if that was all that it had been. But he'd pushed to see her again, and while he didn't regret it for his own sake, he regretted that now Sharon's name was liable to be dragged through the mud with his.

He could already imagine the kinds of things that people would say about her—that she was a whore, or a slut, or at the very least that she was an uncaring person who'd gotten her boyfriend kicked out of his job.

Ross gently ran his fingers over the lines of her face. How could someone that he had known for only six months come to mean the world to him? He recalled their first meeting. Back then, he had certainly desired her, but he'd felt nothing beyond that. He had picked apart her sexual tastes pretty damn quickly (a point of pride for him), but he hadn't known who Sharon was at her core, nor had he cared. How could he possibly have guessed then that she would become so important to him? When he looked back on that night, it felt like he was looking at two completely different people. She had been a stranger, and he had been someone who wouldn't even let his one-night stand stay the night. Now he couldn't even imagine life without Sharon.

He kissed her softly on the cheek and then left her to sleep, closing the bedroom door so she wouldn't disturbed. Jonas came up to him, coat on and car keys in hand.

"I know you'll kick their asses tomorrow," he told Ross, holding out his hand for Ross to shake. "Or, Deb'll kick their asses for you. One or the other."

Ross laughed, and Jonas gave him a quick hug. "Take care of yourself," Ross told him. "Drive safely."

"Or, you know, don't," Leticia said. "You might get a hot surgeon to operate on you."

"Sharon and I are horrible examples and you should under no circumstances follow our lead," Ross said, trying to sound stern but obviously failing given the smiles everyone was flashing at him.

Jonas gave everyone a last wave, and then he was out the door. Debbie gestured to the papers on the coffee table, which Tom was now dutifully typing up on to the computer so that they were organized for tomorrow. "Shall we?" She asked, and although she was currently wearing a Star Wars shirt and ratty jeans, in that moment, she sounded so much like a lawyer that she might as well have been in a courtroom.

Ross sat with Debbie all night, going over what to say and what questions he would probably be asked. Leticia and Melanie acted as the board, firing questions at him and trying to twist his words, while Ross struggled to keep his cool and make sure that nothing he said could be twisted into something else. Tom, valiantly subbing in for Debbie's irreplaceable paralegal, finished typing and printed out a 'case file' with all of the facts and paperwork.

The file contained the 'for sale' listing for Ross's apartment, which he thankfully owned outright so he didn't have to meddle with his landlord about it at two o'clock in the morning. It included the paperwork showing that Ross was co-signed on the lease for Sharon's apartment. There was testimony from Leticia, Sharon's timeline of events, and testimony from Amanda's coworkers about Amanda's willingness to twist facts and go to unscrupulous lengths for a good story. Melanie, as a registered therapist, had given a professional assessment of Amanda's character and abusive behavior, and had gotten her journalist friend to prepare to a counter-story to Amanda's for publication. Debbie also had a copy of Sharon's hospital records, emailed to them by someone in the records department, showing that Sharon had only met with Ross once for a follow-up checkup after the operation.

"Any other character witnesses that we can produce?" Debbie asked.

"There's my staff," Ross said, "And my other coworkers, but they'll have already been interviewed by the board for this."

"Then we'll just have to hope that they gave you favorable reviews," Debbie said.

He hadn't gotten a wink of sleep by morning, but he felt a lot more prepared than he would have if he'd just gone home and passed out for the night. His original plan had been to skip over preparing a defense and go straight to looking for job openings at other hospitals in the Pittsburgh area. But this, this was much better.

At some point, Leticia shoved him into the shower—literally—and Tom and Melanie went home. The shower did wonders for his exhaustion, which he had felt creeping up on him as he might feel a migraine. Leticia helped him pick out a suit and promised to watch over Sharon while he and Debbie headed down to the hospital's administration building.

Ross had been to this building only once before, so he was unfamiliar with it, but he could have sworn that it hadn't looked so imposing the first time around.

"Just out of curiosity," he asked, as he and Debbie entered the building, "What were you guys planning to do since you didn't think I'd be going back to Sharon's last night? Were you just going to show up at my hearing like in a dramatic legal film?"

"Of course not," Debbie said, snorting. "We were going to show up at your apartment and bang down the door."

Ross snorted. The image of all of them knocking on his door until he woke up and then invading his house was an amusing one, but he suspected it would have just been Debbie with the case file, ready to go. Melanie had, at some point, disappeared during the night and returned with a suit from Debbie's apartment. Under any other circumstances, Ross suspected, at least one other person in the room would have pointed out that Melanie had a key to Debbie's apartment, or at least knew where a spare was hidden. It seemed like the sort of observation that would have prompted a lot of talking and teasing. But given that most everyone had been too distracted by hearing preparations to have noticed Melanie's absence until she returned with Debbie's suit, it went without comment.

Now Debbie was dressed for court, complete with a severe bun, just the right amount of makeup, and shoes that made a suitably intimidating clip-clop sound on the tiled floor as they walked towards the elevators.

"This isn't going to be like court," Ross warned her. "It's not going to be a big fancy room with a judge and all of that."

"If that's what you think all courtrooms are like," Debbie said mildly, "Then you're going to be very disappointed when you get called in for jury duty."

They took the elevator up, and Ross tried very hard not to look like he was sweating. He could feel it, in his armpits and at the small of his back, but he at least hoped that he didn't look it. It was a good thing that he had basically moved in with Sharon already, because most of his clothes were with her, and he could pick whichever suit he liked. It would have been just his luck if someone had noticed that he had shown up to his hearing in the same clothes he wore yesterday.

"Just breathe," Debbie advised him. "And follow my lead, all right?"

Ross nodded. Breathe, and let Debbie take the lead. He could do all of that, in theory. It was just that the breathing part seemed a little difficult for him at the moment.

They got off the elevator and entered a large meeting room. The doctors-slash-administrators that served as the medical review board were already present, which Ross had expected. There was Dr. Perry, a gentle looking woman with a soft and rhythmic voice. Ross had met her a few times at parties but had never had the chance to work with her. She seemed to take the lead on most of these things, or so Ross had been told. Besides her there was Dr. Levine, a shriveled-looking man who had been one of the leading neurologists in his day, and was also said to be very tough about the cases he reviewed; Dr. Yusif, who had dark, piercing eyes and had always given Ross the impression that he could stare into your very soul; Dr. Martinelli, a man close to Ross in age, who was head of the maternity ward and also—or so the nurses had told Ross—a terrible flirt, so Ross didn't see why on earth the man should have a problem with him; and finally Dr. Glass, a stern woman whom Ross had run into a few times, and who had always given him the impression that she had just eaten a lemon, and that she hated him for no apparent reason whatsoever.

But then, he could have just been projecting.

"Dr. Hardwick," Dr. Levine said, turning to face him as he entered. "Thank you for coming to see us today on such short notice. And who is this?"

Ross shook each doctor's hand in turn. "This is Debbie Montgomery, my attorney."

"Your attorney?" Dr. Yusif looked at the others as if to check that they, too, had heard what he just had. He then looked back at Ross. "I wasn't aware that you felt that this was necessary."

"Given the severity of the slander and libel my client has been targeted with, we felt that it was best that I attend," Debbie said, in a sharp, no-nonsense voice that Ross had never heard from her before. He almost gaped at her in shock, and then realized that would probably not help matters much, and instead quickly sat down.

"Libel?" Dr. Yusif said again.

Ross looked over at Debbie, who remained standing while all of the doctors sat.

"Yes, libel," Debbie said, her tone just shy of reproaching. "A jealous and abusive ex-girlfriend of my client has published a false, defamatory story in order to disgrace my client, and I find it appalling that you have taken these charges seriously."

"We are required to review all such charges against our employees," Dr. Glass said, her voice as sharp as her name. "We are in a business that requires a deft hand, Ms. Montgomery, and at no time can we risk one of our own overstepping their bounds."

"Of course, doctor," Debbie said smoothly, her voice giving no indication that she was actually backing down or apologizing. "Nobody is suggesting that you should not carry out your duty. But it's interesting, is it not, that my client was only given a twenty-four-hour notice of this hearing? Surely that goes against protocol."

"Given the high-profile nature of this case and the amount of media coverage it has received, we felt it best to act quickly."

"The amount of media coverage?" Debbie sounded delighted at that, and quickly pulled out her phone. She tapped at it for a moment, and then turned it to show the screen to the other doctors. "I just ran an internet search for this story, and it seems that despite the high-profile nature of this case, the media has skipped this one."

The doctors didn't look at each other but Ross could sense that they wanted to. They shuffled in their seats, already a little uncomfortable. Good.

"And what's this about an ex-girlfriend?" Dr. Martinelli asked.

"Amanda Sorrens, who wrote this piece," Debbie said. "She's an ex-girlfriend of my client's. If you would be so kind as to read this report, given by a licensed therapist with knowledge of Ms. Sorrens."

Debbie produced Melanie's report. Clever phrasing, that, Ross thought. Debbie hadn't outright said that Melanie had met Amanda, so Debbie wasn't lying, but she'd given the impression with her tone and choice of words that Melanie had, in fact, met Amanda and knew her.

"I can't betray patient-doctor confidentiality, of course, as I'm sure that you all understand," Debbie went on, "But I hope that the information given in the report there is enough to sketch for you an idea of the kind of person that Amanda Sorrens is."

The doctors all looked over the report, whispering to each other in tones too low for Ross to catch.

"I also have the copy of the report—if one can even call it that—made by Amanda Sorrens for the paper. I've highlighted the factual inaccuracies, if you'd care to take a look." Debbie held up said paper, as if it was a dog treat and she was trying to get them all to sit and be good boys.

"We will take a look, thank you," said Dr. Perry, "But perhaps we can go over the list of reasons why we're having this meeting."

"You're having this meeting because my client has been accused of having an affair with a patient, which is against the Hosptial's code of conduct." Debbie said, flicking some imaginary lint off of her jacket sleeve.

"The charges against Dr. Hardwick are quite serious," Dr. Perry said, her gentle voice quite at odds with her words. "Unless you can provide proof that Dr. Hardwick and Miss Talcott's affair did not start while he was still her doctor—"

Ross felt anger start to bubble up in his chest. He and Sharon weren't having an affair, dammit. He wasn't some married guy who was banging the yoga instructor or the live-in nanny. "I'd appreciate it if you didn't call my relationship with my fiancée an 'affair,'" he cut in, unable to stop himself. "It's a much more serious relationship than that, I can assure you."

All of the doctors looked surprised. Dr. Perry looked over at Dr. Levine, as if silently asking him if he'd known about this, and how he had failed to alert her of it. Dr. Levine shrugged, his eyebrows raising.

"Oh, were you not aware of that?" Debbie asked. "My client and Miss Talcott got engaged last week."

Actually, it was two days ago, but Ross wasn't going to correct

Debbie on that one. And there was no way for any of the doctors to find out that Debbie was lying at that moment. Nobody except for the gallery owner, Tom, and Leticia had known about the engagement beforehand, and the doctors certainly hadn't interviewed any of those three.

"So if it's not too much trouble," Ross said, trying to keep the anger out of his voice, "I'd like it if my relationship with Miss Talcott was treated as serious and long-lasting, rather than a sordid fling to hide in the closet."

The doctors all looked at Ross, and Ross looked right back at them. It was like a kind of staring contest, or like they thought they could read his mind if they just stared at him for long enough. He just hoped that he looked calm but solemn, rather than like he might throw up, which was how he felt inside.

"This doesn't change the fact that we must handle the charges brought against Dr. Hardwick," Dr. Perry said finally, turning to look at Debbie. "Given that this story is in print, people may read it and assume—"

"I understand," Debbie said, smoothly cutting over Dr. Perry, "but you must admit that this is little more than gossip-mongering."

"We cannot ignore the fact that Dr. Hardwick operated on someone with whom he had a personal relationship," Dr. Perry noted.

"I regret that I did not recognize Miss Talcott at the time," Ross admitted. "It was an unfortunate lack of observation on my part. But I immediately handed her over to Dr. Chavez and made no overtures while she was under my care in the hospital."

Just when she came in for a checkup, his brain reminded him, but he wasn't about to mention that.

"If you'll look at the timeline here, supplied by Miss Talcott and verified both by her assistant and by her friend, both of whom served as caregivers while Miss Talcott had limited movement," Debbie said, producing more carefully-typed pages for the doctors to look at, "you'll see that Dr. Hardwick had hardly any role in Miss Talcott's recovery. The majority of her care was done by attending nurses and by Dr. Chavez once she started her physical therapy. I have a statement from Dr. Chavez as well, testifying to my client's good character and stating that he did not pay repeat visits to Miss Talcott while she was undergoing therapy."

Again, Debbie used careful wording to avoid admitting that Ross had visited Sharon once while she was with Chavez. 'Repeat visits' was technically true in that he never repeated his visit to her there, but when phrased that way it sounded like Ross had never visited her at all.

The faces of the doctors showed nothing. Ross had no idea what they were thinking, or if they were thinking anything at all. Perhaps they had already made up their minds about him and this was just a formality. Perhaps he was already as good as fired, and this was just their way of following procedure so that he wouldn't sue them when the axe fell.

"I have more paperwork for you to look at, if you're in doubt of the seriousness of my client's relationship with Miss Talcott," Debbie said, producing the last of the papers. "These statements should show the co-signing of an apartment together, as well as my client listing his own apartment as for sale. Here are some financial statements…"

"We are aware that Dr. Hardwick paid for Miss Talcott's surgery," Dr. Glass cut in.

"That he did, and it was a very generous thing to do," Debbie said. For the first time, he saw Debbie's calm demeanor fracture just a tad. Her eyes narrowed, as if she was sniffing out blood.

"Perhaps," Dr. Martinelli said casually, as if they were discussing where to eat lunch, "Or perhaps it was a form of payment—to buy her silence about their affair, or to convince her to sleep with him."

Ross almost burst out of his chair to punch the guy. "Maybe that's what you would do, or have done," he snapped, "But that's not what I do. I take care of the people that I love, and that's what I was doing."

"Ross," Debbie said, her voice sharp in warning.

"Did you just accuse me of potentially having affairs with my patients?" Dr. Martinelli said, his voice going rough and dangerous.

"Seeing as you just accused me of literally bribing a woman to have sex with me, yes, I think I did," Ross replied, letting his voice pitch low. He would take this out to the street if he had to. Sharon would never, in a million years, let anyone bribe her into doing anything that she didn't want to do—her honor could never be bought. Hell, she'd read him the riot act for paying for her surgery and trying to buy her dinner when he was genuinely just trying to apologize. He pitied the man who tried to silence her on an issue of morality. The poor guy would find his head bitten off at the very least.

"Accusations of prostitution and bribery against my client will not be tolerated," Debbie said calmly, and something about her manner made Dr. Martinelli back off. She was still standing, and was in fact now moving to stand behind Ross. She was the only one one on her feet while everyone else sat, forcing them to look up at her. It was a subtly protective gesture towards Ross, but a threatening one for everyone else. Ross remembered what someone had said the night he'd met Sharon's friends—they'd called Debbie 'our little shark.' There was something very cold-blooded and soulless about Debbie now, something predatory and dark, and it made Ross very, very glad that she was on his side.

"We've spoken with the hospital staff," Dr. Perry said, her voice taking on a tone that Ross remembered his mother, as well as his grade-school teachers, using from time to time. It was the 'settle down or I'll make you settle down' voice. She pulled some papers out of a file and perused them quickly, as if to jog her memory. "They all went on record to say that your behavior was exemplary. No signs of any improper conduct towards a fellow employee or a patient, and none of them remember you behaving inappropriately towards Miss Talcott."

His staff was loyal, thank God. Ross made a mental note to give them all absolutely fantastic Christmas presents this year.

"In fact," Dr. Perry continued, "I had to remind them as to who Miss Talcott was, which I suppose shows that you must have behaved. If you hadn't, then I imagine they would have remembered the patient you misbehaved with."

"I don't think we need to delve into speculation," Dr. Glass said, "Do you?"

"Seeing as Ms. Sorrens' article, upon which you have built your case, relies almost entirely upon speculation," Debbie said sweetly, "I don't see why you're objecting to it now. Seems a bit late for that, doesn't it?"

Debbie gave the doctors all a smile that could only be described as cold-blooded. Oh yes, Ross thought. She was a shark.

"Of course," Debbie added, "If the papers in front of you aren't enough to convince you of the upstanding moral character of my client, the seriousness of his relationship with Miss Talcott, and the unsavory nature of the woman who wrote this article on him, perhaps I can get one of Ms. Sorrens's colleagues on the phone. They have said that they would be delighted to tell you all about the stunts she's pulled over the years."

One of Debbie's hands dropped down to Ross's shoulder, squeezing lightly. That was the cue that she had worked out with Ross beforehand. He spoke, keeping his voice as calm as possible. It wasn't easy, considering how much he still wanted to give voice to the rage he could feel burning like fire in his lungs.

"Dr. Perry—everyone—please understand, I waited until Sharon was no longer my patient to date her. And I am dating her. In fact, we're engaged. This isn't an affair or a seduction. This is a serious long-term relationship. I fully admit that there is the unfortunate coincidence of my operating on her right after we had met, but I behaved as ethically as I could from that moment on, and so did she. There's no scandal here. And if you throw me under the bus, all you'll do is give reporters like this one permission to turn other people's lives into a nine-day sensation. If we give them an inch, they'll take a mile, and how many lives will be ruined because of that?"

Debbie squeezed his shoulder again, this time as a silent *well done*, and Ross let out the breath he'd been holding.

The members of the board all looked at each other. None of them said anything, although both Dr. Levine and Dr. Yusif nodded as if in agreement with an unspoken comment. Then, almost as one, they all turned back to look at Ross.

Ross held his breath.

"You've given us quite a lot to think about," Dr. Perry said at last. "We will review the files that Ms. Montgomery has been so kind as to provide us with, and we will consider what you have said. If you'll step outside, we will have an answer for you shortly."

"Thank you," Ross said, standing.

Debbie nodded at each doctor in turn, and gave them another one of those sweet, terrifying grins. "I'm sure that you'll all make the right decision," she said. "After all, it would be terrible for you to fire an innocent man, or for that information to be leaked to the press. If you're looking for all of this… how shall we put it… kerfuffle, to die down, then perhaps quickly firing a man without giving him due course isn't the way to do it, hmm?"

The five doctors stared at her with equal parts fear and anger in their eyes. Debbie then dropped her file on the table. "Silly me, almost forgot the last file. You'll want to review this, as well."

She then put an arm lightly around Ross's shoulders, like he'd seen security guards do to celebrities, and steered him out of the room.

"What was in that file?" He whispered to her the moment that they were out the door and into the hallway.

"A news article written by another person who works for Amanda's paper," Debbie replied, leading him to a bench. "There are two pieces, actually. It seems that her fellow journalists have been waiting a long time for a chance to cut Amanda down to size. She's loathed by the entirety of the Pittsburgh press. The first piece tells your side of the story and denounces the board for firing you, and the other one is an exposé on Amanda, complete with interviews by the people that she's screwed over."

Ross gaped at Debbie. "You literally just threatened them, you know that, right?"

"Did I?" Debbie replied, examining her perfectly manicured nails. "Or did I merely suggest what the consequences of their actions would be if they pursued a particular course? Consequences are neither good nor bad, they are simply a result of one's actions. Like the law of gravity."

She sounded so completely different from the enthusiastic, geeky person that Ross knew that he lost all power of speech for a moment. When he got his voice back, he said, "You know, you and Melanie are a lot more alike than I thought you were."

"That's what everybody says," Debbie mused.

"Do you think that they'll clear me?" Ross asked.

"If they don't," Debbie said, her voice and face going dark with anger, "They're going to find themselves in the middle of a storm that they're not prepared to weather."

"It's really sweet of you," Ross admitted, "Doing all of this. You really didn't have to."

"I know that I didn't," Debbie replied. "And neither did Mel or Tom or Letty or Jonas. But we wanted to, because Sharon's our friend and so are you. That's just how this whole love thing works."

"I still don't know if I made the right decision," Ross admitted, "Dragging her into this."

"You didn't drag her into anything," Debbie said. "She walked into it of her own free will. Sharon's a big girl, and she's got a good head on her shoulders. Nobody can make her do anything that she doesn't want to do or doesn't believe is right. You of all people should know that."

"I do know that," Ross protested. "I just… I spent so long in love with someone who manipulated me into doing whatever they wanted, even if it made me unhappy. I don't want to do that to her."

"Sharon loves you enough to tell you if she doesn't want to do something, or if she's feeling unhappy," Debbie pointed out. "When we really love someone, we love them enough to be honest with them and deal with any problems that arise, because we know that their love is worth fighting for."

Ross hadn't thought about it that way. "That was… pretty wise of you."

Debbie smirked at him. "I do have my moments."

Ross's phone went off, and he pulled it out of his pocket. It was a text from Sharon. He read it, then looked over at Debbie. "Sharon's here. She's in the lobby."

"Don't tell her where you are. Say that you'll come and see her once this is all finished," Debbie replied. "I know that you want to see her now, but you can't afford to be distracted, and I don't know if the board will look favorably on her visiting you here."

"Fair enough," Ross said, although he didn't like it. He texted Debbie's advice to Sharon.

No worries, Sharon's reply read. *I'll be down here whenever you get finished.*

As Ross finished reading the text and put his phone into his pocket, Dr. Yusif emerged from the meeting room. He looked Ross straight in the eye for a moment, as if he were reading something hidden in there, and Ross wondered again if the guy was psychic or something.

"We're ready for you," Dr. Yusif said after the moment had passed.

Ross and Debbie both stood up. Debbie adjusted her suit slightly. "Shall we?" She said, gesturing at the door to the room.

They filed back in. It looked like the other doctors hadn't so much as shifted in their chairs or touched the papers in front of them.

Ross sat down, and this time Debbie did as well. Her expression was somehow blank and quietly confident at the same time, as if confidence was merely her baseline. She looked so unconcerned that she could have been waiting to hear a weather report for the day instead of the results of a hearing she'd spent all night preparing for. Ross wished he could look like that. He tried for earnest and focused instead, but was a little worried that he simply came off as desperate.

"We've reviewed the papers and discussed the matter among ourselves," Dr. Perry announced. "Your case was quite compelling, Dr. Hardwick, and I must admit it was in no small part helped by your sterling career at this hospital so far."

Ross felt a little like punching the air in victory, knowing that all of his hard work over the years had been noticed and was now paying off.

"There was much debate," Dr. Perry admitted, and Ross saw Dr. Glass and Dr. Levine exchange hostile looks, giving him the suspicion that they were on different sides of the argument, "But in the end we came to a consensus. We find, Dr. Hardwick, that you conducted yourself in an ethical manner as regards to Ms. Talcott," Dr. Perry announced. "You are dismissed."

Ross did his best not to run out of the room. They'd done it! He was okay! He got to keep Sharon and continue his life's work.

Debbie stood, smiling at each of them. It was a much softer and more genuine smile than the one she'd given them before. "Thank you so much for your time, all of you. We hope that you have a pleasant day."

She guided Ross out of the room once more, all the way to the elevators, and did not release him until they were inside.

Then she whooped, taking off her jacket as if she felt constricted by it. "We did it!"

"No, you did it," Ross replied. "You and all of the others. I was going to walk in there completely unprepared and would probably have gotten slaughtered."

"You wouldn't have. Your speech at the end there was perfect," Debbie replied.

"I owe you all for this one," Ross said seriously.

"No, you don't," Debbie said. "You really don't. Unless you want to buy us all a round of drinks tonight, in which case, don't let me stop you."

They exited the elevator and Ross's eyes immediately found Sharon, who was sitting on one of the benches in the lobby. She looked worried, chewing on her bottom lip and fiddling with her hair. She caught sight of them and stood, her eyes wide with worry. "Well?"

Ross managed to keep his face serious for one moment, and it looked like Sharon might burst into tears again—but then he grinned.

"You asshole," Sharon said, laughing. "You had me worried!"

Ross scooped her up in his arms and whirled her around, which got Sharon laughing even harder. "People will stare!"

"Let them stare," Ross declared. "We can be as obvious as we want now."

He did put Sharon down, though, which was when he saw the teasing look in her eyes "What is it?"

"My mom called while I was waiting for you. And I realized that… we're engaged… and you still haven't met my parents."

Ross groaned. "This'll be a shock for them."

"They'll love you, don't worry. After all, I do." Sharon kissed his cheek.

Ross smiled down at her. "Good, since I love you."

"If you two are finished being in love and sickeningly cute," Debbie said. "Can we get lunch or something? I'm starving and neither Ross nor I have slept in twenty-four hours."

Ross laughed, releasing Sharon only to take her hand in his. He didn't know if he'd ever let go. "All right, come on, lunch is on me."

"You're damn right it is," Debbie muttered, but Ross caught her smiling fondly at them when he wrapped an arm around Sharon's shoulders and she let him kiss the top of her head.

He couldn't wait to see what the next six months held, and the six months after that, and the six months after that.

EPILOGUE

Sharon heaved a sigh of relief as she finally got a chance to sink down into a chair. Between getting ready, the vows, the reception line, and dancing, she'd been on her feet all day.

Everything had gone more smoothly than she'd hoped. She had, admittedly, been fretting a lot over the past month as all their planning had finally come together and the big day had approached. Leticia had done a lot to alleviate her stress, booking the church and reception area, organizing the menu, and so on. Sharon didn't know what she would have done without her—and yet she'd continued to worry.

"It's our job to worry," Leticia would say, running around and making sure that the bows on all of the chairs were straight and properly tied. "You just get to sit and look pretty."

Melanie had helped Sharon write her vows. Tom might have been the artist, and Debbie had a way of using words as weapons to get her way in a court room, but Melanie was the one who really understood people and knew what they would want to hear on a day like this.

Getting ready to walk down the aisle, Sharon had been so nervous that she'd thought that she might throw up. Which would have been ridiculous. She'd been dating Ross for over a year and a half. She knew that she loved him. So why was she so nervous?

Perhaps because this felt so official, and everyone had their eyes on her.

"You know," her father said mildly from where he was standing to one side, ready to offer her his arm for their walk down the aisle, "Your mother and I have been through a lot together."

Sharon nodded. Financial troubles, alcoholism, losing their daughter to distance and bitterness and then rebuilding their relationship with her… She had seen her parents go through a hell of a lot together, and she knew that no matter how much of it she actually saw, there was so much more that went on behind closed doors.

"But we made it," her father pointed out. "I never once stopped loving her, no matter how bad things got."

"Even when you two were having screaming fights and she purposefully broke your favorite coffee mug?" Sharon asked. The mug in question had been a gift from her father's father, Grandpa Talcott, and was one of the few things that he'd had to remember him by.

"Even then," her father assured her. "And we had no idea what we were doing when we started out. You and Ross, you're older. You've already got yourselves sorted out. You're successful, you've got a place to live, good friends… You've got so much more than your mom and I did when we walked down the aisle. If we made it work, then, well, I figure you two have got a hell of a good chance."

"And you and mom like him, right?" Sharon asked.

She was pretty sure that her parents had taken to Ross immediately, although they'd been a bit upset that Sharon had gotten engaged to a man and they'd known nothing about it. She just wanted to hear it, one more time. She wanted to know that her parents thought that she'd made the right decision.

"Of course we like him." Her father laughed. "We wouldn't be here if we didn't. But more importantly, he understands you. You two are in sync. None of your previous boyfriends were like that. It almost makes up for you getting engaged so quickly without telling us about him."

"I'm never going to live that down, am I?" Sharon asked, smiling in spite of herself.

"Nope." Her father winked, and then the music swelled and they started their Father and Daughter walk down the aisle.

She might have been a nervous wreck all through the planning process, but all of her concerns about whether the cake would arrive, and if the guests would like the band, and if she would trip in her heels, all faded away once she was standing on the altar with Ross.

They took each other's hands, and repeated after the minister, and then it was time to say their vows. Ross went first. He looked into her eyes and squeezed her hands, and in that moment, everything else fell away. She didn't remember or think about the reception to come, or all the planning that had gone into this, or how she'd been saying that they should have eloped to Fiji and been done with it.

All that existed was Ross, staring into her eyes, looking at her with such love that it made her knees almost give out and her stomach turn to mush.

"Sharon, from the moment I met you, you have been an exception. You put your trust and faith in me from the start, and I can't express how humbled I am by that. I aspire to your level of love, respect, and consideration. I know that I'm not always the easiest person to handle, and I know that I had a lot of baggage going into this relationship. But you didn't let any of those things or people get in the way and you stuck by me, even though I know that it was hard for you. You scolded me when I needed it, but you never made me feel ashamed when I was struggling. You're patient—probably more than I deserve—and you're the sweetest person I've ever met. You spend every day with conviction, dedicating yourself to encouraging people to help chip in and change a person's life. If that doesn't describe a hero, then I don't know what does. You make me feel safe and loved. If I can make you feel half as loved, then I'll feel I have succeeded as a husband and a partner."

Hours later, she could still hear those words ringing in her head. She didn't think she would ever stop hearing them, or seeing Ross's dazzled smile as he watched her walk down the aisle. Hearing them in the moment had made her tear up.

"Ross," she had replied, "I can't say that you've always made loving you easy. But then, I don't think anyone has ever truly made love easy for anyone else. You made me earn every part of you, and honestly, I am so glad of that. I know that I love you and that you love me, without a shadow of a doubt. When you proposed, I knew that you weren't just letting yourself get swept up in the moment. I knew that you really, really knew what you were doing and that you were sure of me. And that faith in me—that's incredible. It means as much to me as holding your heart.

"I love how protected you make me feel. I love that you want to take care of me and that you're willing to take risks for me. I love that you're stubborn. I love how you dedicate your life to saving the lives of others, and how much you care for each and every patient that you help. You routinely put your patients before yourself, and you're such a hero to me for that. You've been a partner from day one and I can't wait to see what the rest of our lives hold together. I love you."

The look of wonder, amazement, and love in Ross's face had made her breath catch in her throat, and she'd seen that his eyes were misty as well.

The rest of the ceremony had passed by in a blur until she was kissing him, holding him close and never, ever wanting to let go. Then Leticia had pulled them apart, laughing and making some joke that Sharon hadn't even registered, and then it was time for the reception. And then, somehow she had ended up here, collapsed in a chair.

She did remember everyone's speeches. Leticia's had started, appropriately, with a story about Sharon at a party in college.

"Sharon was always a responsible girl," Leticia had said. "She was dancing on the table, sure, but she'd taken her heels off and wasn't holding any alcoholic beverages, so I knew right away, this girl was a step above the others. A real sensible type."

Sharon had buried her face into Ross's shoulder, feeling mortified.

"But it turned out that Sharon was very responsible," Leticia went on. "So responsible, in fact, that she wouldn't have flings. Nope. Not one drunken mistake, not one ill-advised hookup, nothing."

"You make it sound like a bad thing!" Sharon protested.

"So when she called me at two in the goddamn morning to tell me that she'd finally had a one-night stand, well," Leticia's trademark knowing smiles flashed across her face, "I knew that this guy had to be someone special. And he was. The moment I met him, I could see that Ross was going to be in Sharon's life to stay. And he hasn't done anything to make me want to castrate him yet, which is more than I can say for Sharon's previous boyfriends."

"Such a low bar," Ross pointed out, and Sharon was obliged to elbow him.

"So here's to Ross and Sharon, especially Ross, for impressing me."

Sharon vowed privately that she was so going to get Leticia back for this when it was time for *her* wedding.

Tom gave a speech as well, as did Debbie. Out of all the friends Ross had met through Sharon, he had grown closest to them. Tom's speech was simple and heartfelt, and Sharon blew him a kiss when he was finished. Debbie's was hilarious and full of geeky references, where she forgave Ross for his inferior taste in Star Trek men, his worrying devotion to Tolkien, and his refusal to let her drag him into the world of video games.

"But don't worry," Debbie assured them all, "He loves Sharon, more than anyone else in this world, and that almost makes up for the rest of it."

Lisa had flown in from England with her husband, and gave a speech of her own, serving as de facto mother of the groom in the absence of Ross's mother.

"Evelyn would have been so proud of Ross," Lisa said. "She was always proud of him, of course, and who wouldn't be with a son like him. But I know that she worried about him, as we all do, when it comes to the love lives of our children. Mine are too young for this, thank God, but there comes a time where you start to worry—will the people we love be taken care of? Will they find that partner to help them get through life when you can't always be there? Will they find someone to see them through the best and the worst? For so many years, Ross was alone, and determinedly so. But then he found Sharon, and well, it was like he was making up for lost time. Everything just fell into place. But that's how it is with the right person. Even when you want to resist it and you work to deny it," and here Lisa had shared a small smile with her husband, and Sharon thought that maybe there was a story there, "it just falls into place, and you know. It did with Ross and Sharon, and for that I am so amazingly glad. He deserves someone who not only loves him unconditionally but challenges him, lifts him up, and makes sure that he keeps being the fantastic, selfless man that we've all grown to know and love. So to the both of you for being there for each other."

Sharon had wanted to hide her face again, this time from an entirely different kind of embarrassment.

Luckily, she wasn't the only one for whom the evening was a blur. "She married me," she'd overheard Ross saying to her father, almost in a daze. "She actually married me."

Her father had just laughed. "That she did, you lucky dog, that she did. You can stop looking like a train ran you over now."

"Trust me," Leticia had told them, "Sharon and Ross were just as surprised to find out they were dating."

Sharon didn't think that she and Ross would ever live that down, but she didn't mind. She had found someone that she loved, someone who helped her to relax and let go. She watched Ross as he danced with her mother. Yes, she thought. She couldn't wait for the rest of their life to begin.

EPILOGUE 2

Ross stared up at the house while Sharon hurried inside. She'd been excited to attend the open house ever since they'd driven past it last week. Ross himself was holding out until he saw the price. He wasn't super enthusiastic about the idea of looking for a house when their apartment already served their needs perfectly well, but the suburbs outside of Pittsburgh were nice, and Sharon wasn't the only one thinking it was time they moved into a place with more room. Jonas and Melanie had both been dropping hints that getting a house was the perfect way to celebrate being married for a year, and Sharon's parents had started asking where the kids were going to sleep.

They had talked about kids, of course, and luckily they were in a good place financially for it if and when it happened. Ross's career wasn't ideal, but then, it never would be. He would always be called into work at odd hours, and there would always be days when he came home and just didn't want to talk—wasn't sure that he was even capable of talking—and would retreat in silence as the weight of another person's life settled onto his shoulders.

But they did both want kids: one, possibly two, hopefully close in age. Sharon had mentioned having one and adopting another, which Ross was perfectly happy with. There were plenty of kids already out there who needed a loving home.

He wondered, idly, if he should ask the realtor about specifically looking for homes that had potential nurseries. Not that he wanted to give her too many ideas. Their realtor seemed almost more eager for them to have kids than they were, and she'd also been pushing the idea of a dog.

"Look at all of this backyard space!" She would exclaim. "Perfect for a kid to run around in with a dog! A retriever, maybe?"

Sharon took it in stride—that is to say, she found it amusing. Ross just wanted the lady to stop planning their lives for them. But hey, she had found them this great house, so he couldn't complain too much.

The house was in the Franklin Park area, a diverse neighborhood that was safe and had a good public school system—not that Ross had been consciously looking into that, or anything, and if he was, well, what was the harm in it? There were plenty of charming houses in the area, but this one he particularly liked. It was on a nice, tree-lined street and had a front porch where they could install a swing.

Ross stepped inside, and took a look around. The house wasn't too large, which was good. He and Sharon might be considering starting a family, but he didn't want them to be swallowed up in a huge house. A bedroom for him and Sharon, a bedroom for future kids, a living room with space for a pull-out sofa in case they had guests, a kitchen with a dining area, and two bathrooms. Perfect. There was also a nice backyard, although possibly not one big enough for a dog. The house didn't have all of the amenities that they wanted—he knew right away that Sharon was going to want to rip up this carpet and put down an entirely new one, and that they would want to see about replacing all of the kitchen appliances—but they could add those things on their own, and everything seemed to be in reasonably good repair.

Maybe Sharon had been right to insist on looking at houses. It was smart to plan for their future, however far away that future might be. And it wasn't like they couldn't afford it, thankfully.

As usual, he felt a pang of sadness at the thought that his mother had never, and now would never, experience this feeling of prosperity. He had been able to give her a taste of financial security before she had died, but he would never be able to give her all that he had wanted to, and all that she had deserved.

Sharon, however, was thankfully still alive and healthy, and she had for some insane reason agreed to marry him. She had even managed to stay married to him for a year now without strangling him, divorcing him, or threatening to do either of the two, and so he was going to seize the opportunities he had with her that he'd missed with his mother.

Ross realized that he had lost track of Sharon, and hurried up the stairs. She wasn't in the master bedroom, but in the smaller one, which overlooked the backyard. There was a tree branch brushing up against the window, and he pointed to it. "We'll have to trim that back," he said. "Can't have any kids sneaking out in the middle of the night to party."

"Oh no, definitely can't have that," Sharon replied, "Especially since both of their parents were known for partying so hard all the time. Such rebels, both of them."

Ross snorted. When it came to their social lives, both he and Sharon had been depressingly sensible their entire lives. "I thought the downstairs was perfect for housing everyone when they come over to visit," he said. "Now that Tom's looking for a place of his own and Mel and Deb are moving in together, we could see about persuading them to move near us."

"We should," Sharon agreed, a conspiratorial glint in her eyes. "They'd be right nearby to play babysitter."

Ross laughed, but was a little confused. "I don't see why they'd need to plan for that just yet, but yeah, I agree, that's definitely convenient. So you like the place?"

"It's perfect," Sharon said, and then grinned excitedly. "I think you should call Maxine so she can talk to whoever's in charge of selling this place. Something this cute won't be on the market for long."

"I agree." Ross came up to stand next to her. "I spoke to the realtor downstairs. She showed me around a bit. The fireplace actually works, by the way. She seemed to like us and she didn't drop any of those not-so-subtle hints about anyone else sniffing around the place, so we might actually get a bid in before others. I think it'll work out."

"Good." Sharon turned to face him, her eyes shining in a way that he loved, "Because I was just thinking this bedroom would be perfect as a nursery."

Ross frowned. "I feel like I'm missing something here. Are you asking to seriously try for a baby?"

Sharon hummed. "We can certainly try for the fun of it, but why would we try to get something that's already on the way?"

Ross gaped at her for a moment in shock, then scooped her up and whirled her around. "Put me down!" Sharon shrieked, laughing. "Ross, careful!"

He set her down as gently as he could. "We're having a baby," he said, knowing he probably sounded just like he had at their wedding when he'd told literally anyone and everyone, *She married me. She actually married me.*

"We're having a baby." Sharon nodded, beaming. "And if it's a girl, I for one say we name her Evelyn. After your mother."

Ross kissed her then and there, just because he could. Perfect.

THANK YOU

Just like getting to the happily ever after, the process of publishing this book required creativity, chemistry, open dialogue, many bottles of wine and putting ourselves out there. We hope you enjoyed the final product.

If you liked the **What's up Doctor** we'd love it if you would be kind enough to take two minutes right now to leave a review. To leave a review simply visit the **book page on Amazon** and click the button that says Write a Customer Review.

If you'd like to read other books by Lacy please sign up at **LacyEmbers.com**

Thank you for joining us on this adventure!

- The Team Behind Lacy Embers

ABOUT THE AUTHOR

Lacy Embers is a collaboration of authors, writers, and editors who love romance novels. Lacy's novels can be relied upon for steamy romance tropes (billionaires, sports stars, happily ever afters), compelling characters and sexy settings. Her books are best enjoyed with a glass of wine.

To learn more about Lacy Embers please visit **LacyEmbers.com**

Made in the USA
Coppell, TX
17 January 2020

14629897R00120